SEDUCED BY THE ALIEN WARRIOR

HOPE HART

CHAPTER ONE

A lexis

I scowl at the massive warriors surrounding us, long, lethal swords in their hands.

"I'm getting really sick of this planet," I mutter.

"Preach," Nevada says.

Don't get me wrong, I'm enjoying the view. I let my eyes linger on the warrior with the dark eyes, who sends me a wink. But I'm tired. Nothing has been easy since the Grivath abducted us, sold us to cruel purple aliens, and crash-landed on this planet.

"State your business," one of the warriors says, his face hard.

"We must talk to Dexar," Terex says, and his voice is calm. *That's right, dickheads. You can't intimidate us.*

Terex is one of the warriors who found us in the clearing while we were mindlessly following the Voildi back to their camp like lambs to the slaughter. Turns out the Voildi were planning to eat us.

See what I mean? Nothing is easy here.

"You have not sent a messenger to request a meeting," the warrior replies, and Nevada gives him a grin. She bares her teeth while caressing her sword, and I smirk as the warriors surrounding us all stare at her like she's a bomb about to go off.

They're not used to women carrying swords here, and they're definitely not used to them wearing leather pants and training with the guys.

"We did not have time," Terex says. "Both of us know that Dexar and Rakiz have formed an alliance. Do you wish to put that in jeopardy with your actions today?"

The warrior narrows his eyes at Terex and waits for a long moment. I almost roll my own eyes. Another man with something to prove. It's the same on every planet.

Finally, he moves to his side, gesturing for us to go ahead. I'm riding with Asroz—one of Terex's buddies—and he keeps the mishua in line as the creature snorts at the other warriors.

Riding a mishua is an adventure in itself. The animals only let warriors ride them, but honestly, I wouldn't want to ride one alone anyway. They're scary as hell.

The animal beneath me is scaled with furry legs. It's like a mad scientist merged a camel and a horse, gave it scales and horns, and painted it green.

Thankfully, Asroz handles the mishua like he's been doing it his whole life— probably because he has— and we make our way into the camp.

Our camp is a couple of days from here. Rakiz is the tribe king, and Terex is in charge of his warriors. He's hot and muscled, and since the moment he met us, he's only had eyes for Ellie, who is currently smiling up at him as we ride through this camp.

I thought Rakiz's camp was large, but this one must sprawl for miles. At the center, a huge kradi stands, at least twenty feet high and the size of a small stadium. This kradi puts the smaller tent-like structures at our camp to shame.

The people here call their tribe king "qatai," and apparently, he's been gradually taking over more and more land since the moment he planted his butt on his throne.

We dismount, and I sigh in relief as I finally stretch my legs. The warriors who found us lead us into the massive kradi, and I gasp, immediately entranced.

My feet sink into thick rugs, and while I expected to be entering a huge, open space, walls have been constructed out of some kind of thick material. One of the warriors lifts a piece of that material, revealing an entranceway.

My geek brain is going nuts for this. There's no way I would've noticed which part of the material wall was the door. This place has been built like a maze, obviously with defense in mind.

Whatever material they've used, it's pretty damn good at soundproofing. As we file into the next room, the sounds of voices almost make me step back, and my mouth drops open.

There must be close to a hundred people in here, all sitting in groups, murmuring at each other as we walk in.

On a large dais, a man sits on a throne, his dark eyes regarding his subjects with what looks like boredom. He raises his head, and my breath leaves me in a whoosh as his eyes meet mine for a single moment.

"Terex," he says, and the murmuring ends.

Nevada caresses her sword again, and Ellie hisses something to her. Likely, she's warning her not to start any shit. Right now, we're completely surrounded on all sides.

"Dexar," Terex nods at him, and the qatai meets my gaze again.

"Who are these females you bring with you?"

The qatai is still staring at me, and if this were any other situation, I'd call him out for being a creeper. I feel the urge to shuffle my feet, and I grit my teeth, staring back at him as he raises his eyebrow.

The man is massive, and a frisson of awareness travels down my spine. His full lips twist as he finally moves his gaze from mine, slowly getting up from his throne and prowling toward us.

I can't help but watch the guy as Terex tells him all about how we ended up on this planet. Not for the first time, I wish we'd been lucky enough to crash-land on a planet like Arcavia, where the Arcav would simply have arranged for us to get on the next ship back to Earth.

But no, we had to land on a backward, barbaric planet where we've already stared down death numerous times. At least we have man candy to perv at along the way, I guess.

The people surrounding us have begun whispering again, and I frown, narrowing my eyes at a woman who seems to be discussing me. In fact, most of them are staring at me, and I have the sudden urge to elbow my way out of this kradi and get the hell away from here.

I get it, I look different. There aren't many people with light hair on this planet, and mine is long and white-blonde. Combine that with light-blue eyes, and I stand out like a sore thumb. Still, the gawking is rude as hell.

I turn my attention back to Terex, who is finally explaining why we're here.

"During the battle, three of the females were taken by

the Voildi. Rakiz has sent warriors to look for them. However, another female also disappeared around the same time. She was small and dark-haired."

A pang of guilt hits me in the gut. *Charlie.* Her name is Charlie, and she was seriously hurt. Her head was dripping blood after we crashed, and once the Braxian warriors killed the Voildi, we searched the surrounding area for her, just in case she'd crawled off somewhere to hide and fallen unconscious.

Finally, Terex and his friends convinced us to leave. We were sitting ducks at that point, and our numbers had already been halved when three of the other human women were stolen by another Voildi pack and Charlie disappeared. He promised us that Rakiz would send warriors to search the area.

Unfortunately, none of those women have been found.

I'm watching the qatai closely, which is why I see the instant recognition in his eyes when Terex describes Charlie. I stare at him, wishing everyone else would disappear so I could shake him until he tells me what I need to know.

Good idea, Alexis. And how do you think your puny human body will move that giant mountain of a man?

"What is your name?" the mountain suddenly asks me, and I frown at him.

"Why does it matter?" Talk about irrelevant details.

I grind my teeth as gasps sound throughout the huge room, and suddenly, the kradi is so quiet that I could likely hear a pin drop.

He stares at me, obviously confused by the fact that I haven't immediately told him what he wants to know.

Get used to it, big guy.

Oh shit. I expected him to glower at me, maybe push his weight around. What I didn't expect was the sudden grin that transforms the hard lines of his face. There are suddenly a bunch of butterflies going nuts in my stomach.

He moves slightly closer, and the light hits his eyes. They're lighter than I thought, but the deep-green color reminds me of sunlight peeking through the leaves of a dark forest.

"You wish for my help, and yet you won't tell me your name?"

Okay, this is getting weird. Why isn't he asking the other women their names? I glance at Nevada, and she has her eyes narrowed at the qatai like he's an unpredictable, dangerous animal.

Glad to know I'm not the only one who's getting weirded out.

The silence stretches, and I blush, annoyed at the number of eyes on me.

"Alexis," I grind out, and his eyes lighten further. I have the strangest urge to punch him and remove some of the satisfaction from his face.

"Alexis," he drawls, lingering over my name. He moves back to his throne and sits, returning his attention to Terex.

"Three nights ago, I received word from a group of my men stationed in the northeast corner of my territory," he says. "I was unsure what to make of their message, believing they must have had too much noptri that night. The female was wearing strange clothes that my men had never seen before and was bleeding heavily from her head."

"Charlie," Ellie murmurs, and Terex wraps his arm around her shoulder. Nevada narrows her eyes at the qatai, and I wish she were closer so I could elbow her. Something tells me that this is a very dangerous man. While he's obviously playing some kind of game, it's evident that he's unused to anyone showing him disrespect.

"And?" Nevada asks.

"And I find myself unwilling to offer up such vital information without anything in return."

"You son of a bitch," Nevada says, and I nod. What an asshole. I wish I could take back all the nice thoughts I've been having about his huge body.

Dexar gets back to his feet, staring at Nevada. My chest suddenly feels tight, and I realize I'm holding my breath.

"What do you want?" Terex asks.

"I want her," Dexar says, gesturing to me, and my breath leaves my chest as I almost choke. I can feel the blood draining from my face. He's joking, right?

"You have *got* to be fucking kidding me," Nevada says, and I nod.

Same page, girl. Same page.

Dexar removes his heated gaze from me and turns back to Terex.

"Your tribe has found three females," he says, and I'm glad we didn't tell him about Vivian, who's hanging out back at camp, just in case Rakiz's warriors manage to find the other women. "You are searching for four more. You are well aware of our shortage of females."

I've got pretty good instincts when it comes to people. Growing up in the foster care system will do that to you. And he may be justifying his assholery, but I don't buy it. I glance at Asroz and move behind him, hoping the giant warrior will protect me if the shit hits the fan.

"You would be safe here," Dexar tells me. "I would see to it personally. No one would harm you, and I will give you the information needed to find your friend."

Charlie. I stare at the ground, a sudden lump in my throat. I'll never forgive myself for not searching for her for longer. Sure, logic said that we had to move on before it got dark, but I still picture her face at night before I go to sleep. Still see her puking in the bushes and walking unsteadily as she suffered through her head injury.

"What kind of person would ask something like this?" Once again, it's Nevada who says what we're all thinking. She's a tough-as-nails marine, and I couldn't be more thankful to have her on my team.

"I am not a good person," Dexar shrugs. "Like most on this planet, I take what I want, and I do not apologize for it. You will need to learn this lesson well if you are going to stay here."

I shoot Nevada a look, which she can't see, but luckily Ellie steps forward and elbows her in the ribs. No point letting the qatai know our plan to get to the crashed space-ship and see if we can fix it. All of us want to go home and resume our lives.

Asroz is still positioned in front of me, and I scowl at Dexar from behind the warrior's back.

Dexar raises one eyebrow, shrugging his shoulders elegantly as if he couldn't care less. But his body holds a strange kind of tension that tells me that my answer is crucially important to him.

Fuck.

My brain begins inventing and discarding options as I search for a way out of this. But there's no logic here, and I attempt to blink back tears as I realize I only have one choice. I glance around at all the people gawking as if we're on a strange, alien reality TV show.

"Out," Dexar instructs, and I meet his gaze again. Instantly, people are up and moving, revealing hidden exits as they leave the large space.

"What is your decision, female?" Dexar asks.

Panic is rising in my chest. I don't want to separate from

the other women. We're like a team. A club filled with the only other people in the universe who know what it's like to be sold on a slave planet only to end up crash-landing on barbaric Agron.

I should never have come to this tribe. And yet what kind of person would I be if I didn't take the chance to help Charlie any way I can? When we get back to Earth, I'm the one who'll have to look at myself in the mirror when I get ready for work in the morning. And it must be hard to meet your own eyes when your cowardice has cost someone their life.

"You won't give us the information any other way?" I ask.

He shakes his head slowly, and I grind my teeth. He's promised that I'll be safe here, but who knows what that even means. I bet his definition of *safe* and my definition of it are not at all the same.

"Don't do it," Ellie murmurs to me. "We'll find another way."

Nevada nods, still glaring at Dexar. "Ellie's right."

I blow out a breath. This decision requires more data. "What does this mean? What exactly do you want from me?"

Dexar shrugs, and I'm once again transfixed by the elegance of the movement. For such a huge man, I'd expect him to move like a brawler. But he reminds me of a lion, slowly stalking across the plains.

And I'm his prey.

"I simply want you here, where I can see you," he says.

I wrinkle my nose, unconvinced, and Nevada snorts. Neither of us were born yesterday.

"Just so we're clear," I say, "I'm not sleeping with anyone."

Dexar grins, and I have to look away. The guy is making

me leave my friends, and yet my thighs just clenched at the beauty of his face. What is *wrong* with me?

"I don't need to make a bargain with you for a tumble. Females beg me for this."

I bet they do. His brow is raised, the look on his face supremely arrogant, and I can practically see women coming to him night and day, fluttering their eyelashes at him, twittering until they get his attention. Strangely, the thought makes my teeth unclench, and I roll my eyes. If he has all these women bowing and scraping, then this isn't about *me* at all. Maybe he's just trying to give Rakiz a giant "fuck you" for some reason, and this is the way he's chosen to do it.

Idiot. In that case, he should've made Nevada stay. Rakiz would probably burn down this world to get her back.

"How long do I have to stay?" I ask. I'm guessing a week or two. Maybe a month. Hopefully by then, the other women will have been found and we can mosey on out of here.

"One revolution," he says, and once again, I can feel the blood leave my face.

Tell me he doesn't mean what I think he means.

"Is that a year? How many days is that?"

"Two hundred and ninety." Dexar says the words as if they don't matter, but all I can see is almost a year of my life, disappearing like smoke.

Nevada and Ellie gasp, and I weigh my options. There's no way I'm staying here that long. This man thinks he has me right where he wants me, but he'll learn. For now, we'll take his information and let him think I'll stay here for a year. But as soon as the other women are found, I'm getting out of here.

I'm the only one who has a remote chance of being able to fix our ship.

I turn to Ellie and Nevada. "Charlie was really hurt, you guys."

Nevada leans forward. "Play the game," she whispers. "I've got your back."

I nod and take a deep breath. "I want one more thing," I say, and Dexar smiles. It's not a nice smile. The lion has me trapped beneath his paw, and he's enjoying watching me squirm.

"What?"

"Rakiz has sent a group of hunters looking for our friends, but they haven't returned. I want you to send some as well. But I want you to swear that if they find them, they'll return them to Rakiz's tribe."

Unlike this motherfucker, Rakiz seems to be trustworthy. Plus, Terex is obsessed with Ellie. He'll make sure the other women are well looked after until I can break my way out of here.

Dexar frowns, and it's like a cloud has covered the sun. Good. Why should I be the only one who's unhappy?

"Why would I do this?" he asks.

"Maybe you're not a good person, but you don't have to be a bad one."

The scowl on his face deepens suddenly, making his face look so dangerous that I find myself stepping back behind Asroz.

Dexar doesn't seem to like this because he steps forward. "Fine, female. Now cease hiding behind another male. I am the only male who will provide you with protection."

Jeez.

"Swear it," I say.

He nods. "You are a brave female. I swear that I will send

my hunters to look for your lost friends, and if found, my men will return them to Rakiz's tribe."

I sigh, suddenly depressed. I got what I wanted. And yet I won't be returning to camp with Ellie and Nevada. Won't be curling up with Vivian in the kradi we've nicknamed the Tramp Tent. This blows.

But at least we'll have a greater chance of finding Charlie. That thought gives me the strength I need to hug Nevada back.

"We'll be back as soon as we find the other women," she murmurs. "Keep your eye on the ball."

I nod. We human women know something that the people on this planet don't. They can separate us, hurt us, steal us, and bargain for us, but we'll come back swinging. And we won't leave anyone behind.

Ellie wraps me in her arms, her face sad. "We'll come back for you," she says, and I grin despite my fury.

"You know, that's what Nevada just said."

I glance at Terex, and he nods. He'll keep the other women safe. I take a deep breath, and then I walk to Dexar's side.

CHAPTER TWO

A lexis

Dexar suddenly looks relaxed, and he gives me a look filled with smug male satisfaction. I tamp down the urge to slap him.

He turns back to Terex. "My men saw the female in the clutches of Dragix as he flew over the Seinex Forest."

From the look on the other warriors' faces, this is not a good thing.

"Who's Dragix?" Ellie asks.

"A giant beast who soars through the sky, breathing fire. Our great ancestor."

Ellie looks visibly shaken. "You're telling me you guys are descended from dragons?"

Dexar frowns, obviously confused by our stunned silence. "Yes. Dragix isn't truly our ancestor, but he is the last of the Great Ones."

Ellie looks like she might pass out, her face drained of all color, and Nevada looks like she's tasting something bitter. Personally, I don't know what to believe. I'd like to think that Dexar is fucking with us. But the other warriors are simply nodding as if it's completely normal that a dragon may have stolen our friend.

"How do we get her back?" Ellie whispers.

Dexar shakes his head, an expression of pity on his face for the first time. "Attempting to find Dragix's lair is suicide."

Ellie ignores this. "Why would a dragon take Charlie? She was wounded. Would he have eaten her?"

I glare at Dexar as he gives another elegant shrug of his shoulders. "The Great One is covetous and possessive. Perhaps she was wearing something that appealed to him."

We were taken in the middle of the night. Most of us were dressed for bed, and I think I would've noticed if Charlie were rocking a massive diamond on her finger or sparkly stones in her ears.

Terex nods, and I shove down the panic that threatens to rise as he and the others get ready to leave. I give Ellie a smile, and Nevada nods at me as they file out.

I'm alone with Dexar, and it feels like every hair on my body is raised in alarm as my muscles tense in awareness. He studies me out of those forest-green eyes, and I examine him back.

"Come," he finally says, his voice echoing in the huge, empty room. "I will show you to your quarters."

I expect him to lead me out of the giant kradi, but instead, he leads me deeper inside it. Guards are positioned throughout, and within moments, I'm completely confused. I'm not exactly great with directions at the best of times, and this space has obviously been designed to befuddle any enemies who think to rush through it.

The dark corridors are narrow, which means anyone

who thought to attack would be forced to line up for the pleasure of meeting the swords of the huge guards who stand at attention as we walk past.

"I'm staying here?" I ask as we continue walking, and the walls of the kradi change from a deep blue to a royal purple and finally, a dark red.

"Of course," Dexar murmurs. "You are my guest."

He says "guest" like he means something else, and I send him a look. The corner of his mouth curls up, and I scowl. At least one of us is having fun.

Dexar stops in front of a gorgeous piece of material in the same ruby color as the walls, but it's intricately woven with some kind of gold thread. He nods to one of the guards, who jumps into motion, lifting the material aside.

"Did your arms break on the way here?" I mutter before I can bite my tongue. The guard's eyes just about pop out of his head, and Dexar turns to look at me. He appears slightly confused for a moment, and then he seems to get the insult, raising one eyebrow.

He smiles, and something tells me that amusement on his face doesn't bode well for me, but he merely lets out a hum and gestures for me to step into the room.

"Wow." I can't help but be impressed. It's about twice the size of the kradi I shared with Vivian, and Dexar nods toward the opposite side of the room, where another piece of material has been tied back.

It looks like it leads to whatever passes for a bathroom in this camp, and I run my fingers over one of the chairs that sit against another wall, surrounded by large, intricately decorated pillows. They've been carefully arranged on a soft blue rug, and I immediately want to sink down on top of them for a nap.

Dexar points to a huge wooden chest sandwiched by two

slightly smaller trunks. "They are filled with clothes, although I will tell the seamstresses to bring more."

"I'm sure that won't be necessary," I say, and he ignores me, striding forward to yet another door, this one hidden away. He pushes the fabric aside and gestures for me to join him.

The bed is huge. Unlike in Rakiz's camp, where we slept on a pile of soft furs, this bed has an honest-to-God mattress. I have no idea what it's filled with, and it certainly doesn't look like the Posturepedic in my apartment at home, but the thick blankets and soft pillows are calling to me.

My eyelids are getting heavy just looking at it.

Dexar shows me a long cord in the corner of the room. And then he pulls it before striding back into what I've mentally dubbed the living room.

Within moments, two Braxian women appear. One of them is older, and I'd assume she's in her sixties if she were on Earth, although who knows how long people live on this planet.

She smiles at me, and I can't help but smile back. She has deep laugh lines around her mouth, and her expression is practically giddy, her eyes sparkling as she looks at me.

The other woman doesn't look so pleased. She's about my age, maybe a few years younger, although I'd put her in her mid-twenties on Earth. She has dark, almost black, hair with a single long white streak at the front. The effect is striking. From the look in her eyes, she's much less impressed with me than her friend seems to be.

Fair enough.

"This is Yari," Dexar says, and the older woman nods at me. "And this is Nara." Nara finally smiles, and Dexar turns back to me.

"Yari and Nara will be responsible for bringing you food,

helping you bathe, and assisting you with anything else you may need."

Servants? I don't think so.

"Oh, that's fine," I say. "I can do that stuff myself."

Dexar ignores me once again, turning to Nara. "I believe Alexis would like to bathe soon. I will send Mena with some more dresses."

I grit my teeth at his high-handedness, but I wait until both women nod and move toward the bathroom.

"I don't need any help with that stuff," I say, and he steps closer.

Oh, he's playing the "get into her space and she'll do what I want" game. *What fun.*

"Regardless, you have it."

Something about the hard look on his face tells me I should pick my battles. I have no intention of being constantly watched while I'm here. If I suddenly need to haul ass back to Rakiz's camp, I have no doubt that both of those women would narc to Dexar in a heartbeat.

But I'll fight with him about it later. For now, I turn away, choosing to ignore him. He wants to boss me around? He doesn't get rewarded with my attention.

The qatai lets out a low growl, and I can hear his overly polished boots meet the ground as he leaves the room, stalking back out into the hall. The guard must drop the material because the room instantly silences.

"Your bath is ready," Nara announces, and I turn. She steps aside, gesturing for me to move into the room, and I freeze, suddenly overwhelmed.

"You must be tired," she says. "The water is warm." Her voice is strangely cajoling, and I smile.

"A bath sounds great."

Yari is waiting for me, and she gestures for me to turn

around. She pulls at the tie on the back of my dress, and I clutch the dress to my chest as it falls open.

"I've got it from here," I say, turning back around.

She frowns slightly. "Are you sure?"

"Yup, I've been bathing myself since I was a kid. I've got this covered." I grin to soften my words, and she looks unconvinced but finally nods.

"I will ensure food is brought to your rooms. If you need anything, please pull the rope in your sleeping room."

"Thank you," I say. "I really appreciate it."

She smiles, her face lighting up. "It's my pleasure. We've been waiting for you for such a long time."

Dexar

I sit on my throne, ignoring the whispers of my court, who have taken their usual places, gossiping amongst themselves.

My mind is on the female with white hair and ice-blue eyes. Finally, she has come to me.

Alexis.

"Qatai?"

I blink, forcing myself to concentrate on the present as Brix steps forward. "Yes?"

"Tazo and his warriors have returned. He brings Zarix with him. Zarix is severely wounded."

I'm on my feet within moments, striding toward the healers' kradi. Zarix is a friend, and I have hope that one day, he will choose to stop punishing himself for a death that was not his to take responsibility for and rejoin my tribe at camp.

For now, his impressive skills at hunting and killing the Voildi have made him perfect for the mission I gave him. Never has he returned to camp seriously wounded.

What could have happened?

I realize I've asked the question aloud when Brix replies.

"He is traveling with a female who looks like those who arrived here earlier, along with a Krinir boy."

I tilt my head. It is well known that a Krinir female and her son are under Zarix's protection, but as far as I'm aware, he's never taken the boy with him. And how did he end up with one of the missing females?

I consider this as I make my way through the camp, Brix by my side and three guards traveling behind us.

The Krinir boy is standing outside the healers' kradi, next to one of the alien females.

"Is he okay?" he asks the female miserably, his lower lip shaking as he hands her a crossbow.

"You heard his friend," she replies gently. "He's too stubborn to die."

The boy nods, but it's clear that guilt plagues him. "This is my fault. I did this."

The female sighs. "You made a mistake. You acted before you fully thought about the consequences of distracting him. That Voildi saw what you did to the first one. He was luring you into a trap."

That explains it. There are few warriors as obsessed with protecting females and children as Zarix. Unfortunately, his obsession manifests as a refusal to be responsible for either, since he is convinced he is unworthy to be trusted with their lives.

"Zarix could die," the boy says.

"He could. But he wouldn't want you to blame yourself. You did something stupid, and now you get to learn from it."

The boy looks unconvinced, shrugging his shoulders and walking away, and I step forward.

"That was what he needed to hear," I say. I smile at the female, and her eyes widen as she balances her weight on one foot. This female has been injured, and I'm suddenly impatient to know exactly what has happened.

"I'm worried about him," she says, and it takes me a moment to realize she is talking about the boy.

I nod. "I will have my people watch him. He can have the illusion of space for now." I glance at Brix, and he nods before turning to speak with one of the guards.

"I am Dexar, the qatai of this tribe," I say.

"I'm Beth."

"Thank you for helping bring Zarix home."

The female's eyes are wet, and she looks away. "I'm partly responsible for his injury. It was the least I could do."

There are no words that will make this female lose the guilt that obviously plagues her. At least none that I can say.

"I will attempt to talk to Zarix now. The information he has is crucial," I say.

"Can I come with you?"

I nod, stepping into the kradi with my guards.

One of the healers glances at me, her eyes widening. "He is conscious now, qatai," she says.

Zarix is lying flat on his back while the healers work on the deep wound in his side. The human female lets out a shuddering breath next to me, and I move closer to the bed.

"Zarix," I say, and he opens his eyes, although it's clear that the movement costs him, and his voice is heavy with pain.

"Tecar's tribe is the first targeted. But that information can't be trusted. Tellou turned on us."

He is a dead male walking. There is nothing I tolerate less than betrayal.

"Just Tellou?" I ask. "Or all of his people?"

He scowls. "All of them. They believe they will fare better under the Voildi. Their people are not hunted for meat, so they have chosen to take their chances as the Voildi's allies."

I grind my teeth but nod. "Anything else?"

"Her leg," he says, nodding toward the female. "She needs a healer."

I gesture to one of the healers, who steps forward.

"Recover well, Zarix," I say. "We will need you."

I stride from the tent, cursing. Beside me, Brix glowers at anyone who so much as looks at him, both of us silent as we reflect on Zarix's words.

The Voildi are a flesh-eating plague on this planet. The fact that they have managed to collaborate long enough to be a legitimate threat to a Braxian tribe is wholly unexpected.

Tecar's tribe is small. The male has no desire for land and seems content to simply rule his modest territory alone. It is difficult for me to understand this contentment, but the tribe king has never been a threat to me and does not produce any goods that are unique enough for a trade agreement.

Unfortunately, his refusal to grow his tribe and territory has made him a target.

We stride into the kradi, and I ignore the Great Room in favor of the small room I use when I want privacy. My father created the Great Room as a way for his people to visibly see their qatai and feel connected to him. While I respect the tradition, all of my most important decisions are made away from prying eyes.

I glance at Brix. "I need to see Tazo."

He nods and stalks away, his expression still dark. Learning that the Voildi are planning to attack a Braxian tribe has shaken the foundation of everything we assumed about the creatures.

I grind my teeth as I sink into my favorite chair, staring at the deep blue of the wall.

"Underestimate your enemy at your peril," my father would say. *"Or they will attack when you least expect it."*

As the qatai of the largest Braxian tribe on Agron, I have failed.

"Qatai." Tazo nods in a shallow bow, and I gesture toward a chair. He sinks into it, his eyes bright and focused on mine.

"Your actions bringing Zarix to camp have saved his life," I say.

The warrior glances away, a muscle twitching in his jaw. Once, the two males were as close as brothers. Now Zarix treats Tazo as if he is barely an acquaintance.

"What did the healers say?" Tazo asks.

"They were working on him. I expect him to be up and on his way to Tecar's tribe within days."

Tazo tenses, and I lean back, raising an eyebrow. "Yes?"

"I would like to go with him."

I nod. "And you will. However, you will have to follow once he has already left."

Tazo rolls his eyes, and despite the seriousness of the situation, I laugh. Zarix is well known for believing the fate of everyone on this planet rests on his wide shoulders. He usually insists on hunting alone.

"Send a messenger once you arrive at Tecar's tribe," I say.

Tazo nods and gets up to leave, and I take a moment to

picture the female currently resting in the qatal's rooms. She is a fierce female, and her actions have proven her to be honorable and courageous. After so long, it is difficult to believe that she is so close.

I have little doubt that Alexis will go to war with me over my plans for her. However, she will find herself outmatched.

The icy-eyed female will never leave my side.

CHAPTER THREE

A lexis

I let my eyelashes flutter and then lower my eyes as I stare at the ground.

I can't quite muster up a tear, but from the sympathy on the guard's face, I look suitably forlorn.

"It's just that...if this is going to be my new home, I should probably see it, don't you think?"

"Uh..."

I move closer, resting one hand on his chest for balance as I peer up at him from beneath my eyelashes.

Poor guy looks like a deer in headlights.

After my bath last night, I passed out before waking early this morning when my stomach was rumbling. I inhaled a tray of fresh fruit, nuts, and bread and then paced, attempting to reconcile myself to my new situation.

You can get through this, Alexis. Look at this shit. Clean water, plenty of food, a comfortable bed. You would've loved this when you were a kid.

Growing up in the foster care system was a real treat. Nothing like being passed from family to family until you finally stop caring that the few clothes you own are once again getting packed into a garbage bag. Eventually, I got numb to it.

As an adult, I can admit that it made me strong. This is just another difficult situation that I need to figure my way out of.

First step? Convincing this guard to give me a tour of the camp.

When I finally peeked my head out of the long piece of material that's used as a door, there was only one guard standing outside.

He's younger than any of the other Braxian warriors I've seen since I arrived, and I half expect his voice to crack. While he's huge and no doubt deadly in a fight, his face lacks the hardness that most warriors seem to have.

"I just have no idea what time it is, you know? I need some fresh air. Maybe you could...*show me* around?"

My hand rises on his chest as he sucks in a breath, and I barely suppress a grin as the tips of his ears turn red.

"Tavis," a deep voice says, and I turn as another guard walks toward me.

I drop back down from my tiptoes and survey the older guard as he stares at me suspiciously.

Not ideal.

This guard gives my new friend, Tavis, a hard look, and Tavis steps back to his spot by the wall.

"Can I help you with something, qatal?"

I frown at that, and the guard seems to catch himself.

"What would you like us to call you?" he asks.

"Alexis."

He hesitates, and I smile. I've got his number. This guard is going to be trouble for me. He's one of those brownnosers who could probably quote from the employee handbook if he were on Earth. Plus, I can almost picture him yelling at me to take off my shoes as I make my way through security at an airport.

He chooses not to repeat my name, and I feel my smile widen.

"And your name?" I ask.

"Rowax."

"Rowax," I purr, and his face stays blank. "I'd really like to go outside. I was wondering if Tavis here could show me around. I'd really...*appreciate* it."

I'm laying it on way too thick, and Rowax raises one eyebrow, obviously not impressed. Tavis, however, blushes so deeply that I could probably cook an egg on his face.

Aw.

"I will take you outside," Rowax says, and I smile brightly, although I'm mentally cursing. This guy is a hard-ass.

"Sounds lovely."

All the dresses in the huge wooden trunk were similar. Thin, gauzy, and mostly brightly colored. The aqua-colored dress I'm currently in is embroidered with the same gold thread that decorates the door to my room. I've paired it with a light cloak and matching slippers, but one thing became clear as I rummaged through the yards of material. There are no clothes that would protect me from the elements if I decided to make a run for it.

I'm obviously expected to be an inside pet.

Good fucking luck with that, Dexar.

I don't know why he wants me here, especially since I

made it clear that sex was off the table. Sure, this tribe may be lacking in women, but I fail to see how one human woman is going to turn the tide.

Then there's Yari's strange proclamation from last night.

"We've been waiting for you for such a long time."

Just what exactly does that mean? When I pressed her, she clammed up and left the room, while Nara stood white-faced and clearly upset in the corner.

This place is an enigma on top of a mystery, with a heaping helping of confusion on top.

I mull this over while Rowax leaves Tavis on the door and leads me out of the kradi. I attempt to memorize the way out, but after a few long minutes of walking and multiple twists and turns, I give up.

"What do you guys do if there's a fire or something?" I ask.

"There are many hidden exits."

Hope sparks in my chest. "Feel like showing me some of those in case I need to get out of here in a hurry?"

One look at Rowax's craggy face and that hope dies.

"You will always be guarded by trusted warriors who know where to find the exits."

I grind my teeth but stay silent as we reach another pair of guards, and Rowax nods to them. One of them pushes open a flap of the kradi that looks exactly like the rest of the material walls, and we're suddenly outside.

We didn't go through the massive room where I first met Dexar. I wonder how many rooms and exits there are in this place. I need some kind of map.

The sun has only recently risen, and while it's warm on my face, I'm grateful for the cloak. Rowax leads me down a long path, and I attempt to ignore the staring. While it's early, much of the camp is already up and going about their lives, and I'm obviously the hot new topic of conversation.

We pass the training arena, which looks similar to the one in Rakiz's camp, only larger. For a moment, I expect to see Nevada taking lessons from Asroz, her sword in her hand and a fierce look of concentration on her face.

In Rakiz's camp, the weapons kradi was located close to the training arena, although not right next to it. I keep my eyes peeled as we wander and Rowax points out crap I couldn't care less about—like the seamstress and food kradis.

Cool story, but where are the weapons at?

"Where are the mishua?" I ask.

Rowax tilts his head and points toward the other side of camp. Just like the last camp, this one is located next to a river, and the mishua are kept close to the water, with the training arena on the opposite side. Dexar's kradi is located smack-dab in the middle of the camp, which is bad news for me if I need to haul ass out of here.

I can't ask about the weapons. If there's one thing I learned at the last camp, when Nevada almost started a riot, it's that females don't walk around armed on this planet.

Rowax is already looking at me with suspicion in his eyes.

"Can we walk around the outside of the camp?" I ask. "I'd like some exercise."

He shakes his head, and I sigh.

"What about a loop inside the camp walls?"

While the Braxian people are mostly nomadic, this camp seems to be more permanent than Rakiz's camp. The walls around it look like stone, for one thing, and I can't imagine them being rebuilt every few months if the tribe is on the move.

But what do I know about a barbaric alien tribe?

Rowax pauses. "I don't suggest you attempt to escape, qa-Alexis," he finishes, looking slightly flustered. Then his face hardens again. "You agreed to stay here for one revolution."

I grind my teeth and look away while I try to keep my cool. "I did." I smile. "And I have no intention of leaving. I just want to get to know my new home."

Rowax doesn't look convinced. He better not be a permanent fixture outside my door. If so, the first thing I'll need to do is somehow arrange for him to be replaced.

Sure, I agreed to stay here. But everyone knows that deals made under duress don't count. I'll stay put for now, but as soon as the other women are found, I need to get my fine ass to that ship.

There's no guarantee that I'll be able to fix it, of course. Sure, I may be an astronautical engineer on Earth, but as we learned when the Arcav invaded, our technology is laughable compared to what they take for granted.

One thing I noticed when we were on that ship? It was practically falling apart. So, even if it *could* theoretically be fixed, the chances aren't great that I would be able to get my hands on the right parts.

I lock that conjecture away in my Vault of Unpleasant Thoughts. No point worrying about it until I can actually see what I'm working with.

"Alexis?"

"Sorry, I was daydreaming. As I said, I really just want to look around."

"It will have to wait," Rowax replies, nodding at another warrior, who has approached while I was woolgathering. "The qatai has asked you to join him for the midday meal."

Alexis

Yari is waiting for me when I arrive back in my rooms, slightly annoyed by Rowax's refusal to show me the things I need to see.

The annoyance is warring with the weird feeling in my chest at the thought of seeing Dexar again. I don't know what he wants with me, but I'm fixated on the confident way he declared that females *beg* him for a "tumble."

Challenge accepted.

No, Alexis. Think with your brain and not with your pussy.

One thing I've learned about sexy, arrogant men? While they can be fun in bed—if they can put their money where their mouths are—they're rarely worth the experience. That arrogance quickly translates into smug self-importance, and before you know it, they're bossing you around, all while standing you up and engaging in some good old-fashioned gaslighting.

No, thanks.

Not to mention, this guy is a king. You know what that means? He's never had to *work* to please a woman. Sure, he may have women falling over themselves to climb into his bed, but once there, I bet they quickly realize that the cake just ain't worth the bake.

I snigger as I imagine him lying on his back, hands folded behind his head as a faceless woman does all the work in bed.

My mind replaces the woman's face with my own, and I shut that thought down.

Nope, nope, nope.

"Did you say something?"

I blink at Yari, who has insisted I change into another dress. I attempted to explain to her that I'd been wearing this one for approximately thirty minutes, but she declared that it wasn't elegant enough for a meal with the king.

The more I learn about this guy, the less I like.

"Tell me about yourself, Yari," I say, desperate to think about anything except sitting across a table from Dexar.

She smiles at me, the lines around her eyes deepening. "What would you like to know? No, not that way. Let me do it."

She brushes my hands aside and ties the new dress at the back. This one is a deep purple, but other than a little more gold sewn into the fabric and slightly longer sleeves, it's almost identical to the one I was just wearing.

"Do you have kids? Children," I clear up when she frowns in confusion.

Her frown disappears. "I do. Three sons, all of them with sons of their own. Unfortunately, none of them have been blessed with daughters."

"That seems to be a problem on this planet."

She nods sadly. "I don't know if my sons' sons will have a chance to find mates. Their generation is the worst yet, with so few females born that our people seem destined to disappear from this planet."

"I'm sorry."

Not for the first time, I wonder what could've led to such a relatively sudden decrease in female babies. Since I'm going to be here for at least a few weeks, maybe I can do some research and leave it with the tribe when I move on. My ego isn't large enough that I imagine I'll be able to solve such a massive problem, but maybe my background in science can help in some small way.

Sometimes, the best breakthroughs come from getting a slightly different point of view.

"I will show you to the qatai's rooms," Yari says.

I nod, and then I'm frowning as Yari heads into my bedroom instead of moving back toward the entrance. I follow her like a lost lamb, and my mouth falls open as she moves her hand, revealing yet another hidden doorway.

This tiny corridor is smaller and more dimly lit than any of the others I've walked down so far. It only takes us a few steps before Yari is showing me another doorway, gesturing for me to step inside.

"I will return to your rooms. Enjoy your meal."

I almost beg her not to leave me as my hands begin to shake. I scowl. Why am I suddenly as nervous as a virgin on her wedding night?

I shake off the nerves and stride through the doorway and into a large room. A long table sits in the middle of the room, with enough space to seat eight people. To the left, Dexar is slouched on a chair that sits low to the ground. His brow is furrowed in concentration as he studies a long piece of paper before rolling it up as his green gaze meets mine.

It's the first paper I've seen on this planet, and my hands itch to touch it. I want to know which material these people make their paper out of, and I'd love to examine the language they write in.

Dexar gets to his feet, and I'm struck by the smooth roll of muscles as he stands. The guy sure is built. But as much as he gives the impression of indolence with his inability to sit in a chair without sprawling in it, I'm not fooled. His body seems tightly coiled, and I have no doubt that he could strike faster than a snake if threatened.

"Welcome," he says.

I don't know what to say, so I shuffle my feet. Something

about him turns me into an uncertain, slightly irrational mess.

We both turn as a bell sounds, and four servants begin lifting trays onto the long table.

"Are you hungry?" Dexar asks.

I nod, still watching as the food is laid out. "I can't possibly eat all that."

Dexar simply smiles, his eyes laughing at me, and I look away.

"Try," he says, striding toward the table. He thanks the servants, and they bow before silently moving out of the room and leaving us alone.

I take my seat, and Dexar places a few things on my plate before doing the same to his own. I reach for a glass of water, wishing desperately for it to turn into wine.

Dexar seems to be okay with my silence, but his steady gaze is disconcerting.

"What?" I ask.

He shrugs. "Do I make you uncomfortable?"

I hate it when people answer a question with a question. Dexar seems to read my mind because a dimple appears in his cheek.

"Yes," I say, and he leans back, running his eyes over me.

I take a bite of some kind of greens. They've been cooked in a savory sauce, and I immediately take another bite. *Yum.*

"I find that I enjoy watching you eat," he says.

As much as I know people, and as good as I am at predicting their behavior, this man is a complete mystery to me.

The scientist in me wants to figure him out.

The woman in me just wants him.

We talked about this, Alexis.

"Why am I really here?" I ask.

Dexar takes a sip of his drink, and I attempt to ignore the way the muscles in his throat move as he swallows.

"I told you. I want you where I can see you."

"You don't even know me."

He shrugs again. "We're getting to know each other now, are we not?"

I try another approach. "One of the women said, 'We've been waiting a long time for you.' What does that mean?"

The qatai stares me straight in the face. "I have no idea."

I'm positive he's lying, but I don't know why.

I stare back at him. "I don't believe you."

"Why would I lie to you?"

"I don't know. You tell me."

I grit my teeth and then force myself to sit back and take another bite. The meat is tender and perfectly cooked, and I attempt to ignore the feel of his eyes on me as I eat it.

For some reason, I can't seem to find the ability to pull my "butter wouldn't melt in my mouth" flirty act with this man. Something tells me he wouldn't believe it even if I tried.

"What do you think of this planet?"

The change of subject isn't exactly smooth, but he's obviously not going to give me any information about why he wants me here.

I shrug, mimicking him, and he flashes his teeth at me as he smiles.

"It's...fine. It's very different to Earth."

"Different how?"

I spend the next few minutes explaining some of the ways my planet works. The qatai can't seem to reconcile the concept of democracy, dismissing the idea with a wave of his hand.

I narrow my eyes at him. "How many people belong to this tribe?"

"Eighty-two thousand six hundred and seventy-one. Seventy-two," he corrects with a smile. "Veris just welcomed a son into the world."

I try not to be impressed with the fact that he knows exactly how many people are in his tribe down to the last birth. "What makes you certain that you should be the one to rule so many people?"

"My father ruled, and his father ruled another tribe before him." His tone changes at the mention of the other tribe, warning me not to press further.

"So just because you happen to have been fathered by a tribe king, you believe you're uniquely suited to decide what's best for so many people?"

He tilts his head. "Yes. I was raised to think about what is best for my people since I was old enough to understand who my father was. Under my rule, this tribe has strengthened, our territory has grown, and no other tribes would dare attack us. My people are happy."

Arrogance coats his words like honey on a knife, and I raise an eyebrow but say nothing.

This seems to frustrate him because he frowns, leaning forward. "Who makes decisions about what actions are best for the people on your planet?"

Never could I have imagined that I'd be explaining the concept of democracy to a tribe king on a barbaric planet. I pinch my thigh under the table.

Ouch. Yup, definitely not dreaming.

"The people elect leaders who they trust to make these decisions for them. They vote for what they want."

"Vote."

I laugh as Dexar mangles the word in English. Obviously, the translator in his ear has failed. There's no word for the concept in Braxian.

He leans closer, giving me a slow smile. "Do that again," he murmurs.

"Do what?" My voice is hoarse. That smile of his...

"Laugh."

I stare at him, confused, and we're silent for a long moment.

"I want to be able to walk around the camp by myself," I say, and his face shuts down. Any hint of humor leaves his eyes, and he becomes the ruthless qatai who negotiated for my lack of freedom.

"No."

"Why not?"

"It's too dangerous."

I take a deep breath. Yelling at him will just erase any ground I've gained during this conversation. Dexar obviously sees me as some kind of bargaining chip. I need to make him understand that I'm a woman.

"Why would it be dangerous?" I ask, genuinely confused.

He glances at my empty plate. "If you're finished eating, I need to meet with my council."

That's it. I push back my chair and get to my feet. "Why are you being so ridiculous about this?"

"Why do you feel the need to wander this camp without a guard?"

I open my mouth, unsure what exactly to say, and he laughs, but the sound is harsh.

"Did you think Rowax would not tell me about your questions?" he asks.

"What questions?"

He tilts his head, looking down his nose at me, and I

fight back the urge to slap him across the face. In this place, hitting the king would probably not be a good idea. They'd probably try me for treason or some shit.

"Why play games? After just one night here, you are already looking to escape. Is honor so meaningless on your planet?"

My mouth drops open, and I lean over the table. "You're saying *I* don't have honor? Are you or are you not the same man who *bargained* with my freedom in exchange for information about my lost, injured friend?"

His face is like stone as he gets slowly to his feet. Then his eyes drop to my chest, and they're hot when they return to my face. I look down and mentally curse. The dress is low-cut enough that I've been giving him a nice view of my cleavage while leaning over the table.

He opens his mouth, and then the damn bell sounds again, turning his eyes blank once more.

"I have a meeting," he says as a warrior appears, bowing at the qatai before glancing curiously at me. Dexar stalks out the door, and I stare at the empty table.

CHAPTER FOUR

D^{exar}

I thought it would be easy. That having the human female in my space would allow me to focus on things that are more important.

Instead, she makes me question things that I have never questioned before.

All while she attempts to manipulate me into letting her study the security of this camp.

I snort.

"Did you say something, qatai?"

"No."

My councillors are silent as we sit in the large kradi they use to gather and discuss issues to bring to my attention. I scan them, reflecting on the female's words.

I am the ultimate authority in this tribe. Yet my council is the closest thing we have to the idea she calls *democracy*.

Such a thing would not work here, where Braxian tribes

have historically been quick to war with each other. However, I still enjoyed watching Alexis's eyes light up as she explained the concept to me.

"We have received word of Lafa's tribe, qatai."

I narrow my eyes, pushing thoughts of the female aside. I find myself wanting to apologize for putting the hurt in her eyes—

"Qatai?"

"What have you learned?" I ask.

Andon straightens. The warrior is younger than most on my council. After he came close to death, his mate insisted that he refrain from battles unless we are at war or he is ordered to fight.

Now he has turned all his focus and attention onto gathering the information that helps me make some of my most important decisions.

"There are reports that Lafa has been seen speaking to the Voildi," he says.

The room goes silent. No Braxian would speak to the flesh-eating creatures. They are vermin of the worst kind, yet they are dangerous vermin.

Many revolutions ago, Tazo's sister left camp alone, planning to follow Zarix after an argument. The Voildi found her before taking her body and leaving behind only enough for us to realize what had happened.

We are not the only tribe to suffer losses from the Voildi.

"Impossible," Orcan snorts. "Never would a Braxian tribe king speak with Voildi."

Andon ignores him, speaking directly to me. "I would not have believed it either, qatai. Yet multiple sources have reported the same. Lafa has not been as careful as he should."

I lean back in my seat as the councillors mutter amongst themselves. Orcan slowly gets to his feet, heaving a sigh.

"If Lafa were planning some collusion with the Voildi, he would be careful not to be seen by anyone. Do we really want to risk what small cooperation we have from Lafa's tribe over these unfounded rumors?"

Andon ignores the older male once again, speaking directly to me. "Not rumors. Facts. Lafa has been seen multiple times with several Voildi. I disagree that the tribe king would be careful. He has gradually lost more and more territory, and his tribe grows smaller as his warriors choose more established tribes. We have welcomed nine of them ourselves in the last few years."

I raise an eyebrow. Andon is proving knowledgeable and capable. I have a feeling that if asked, the male would be able to name all these warriors along with any others who have sworn loyalty to our tribe over the past years.

I can name the few warriors who have left. Varic's face swims in my mind, and I push it away.

"Paranoia," Orcan snaps, and the warriors next to him nod in agreement.

"What you call paranoia, I call preparation," Andon says softly.

"Listen, you—"

"Enough," I bite out.

The room is silent while I think. Over the past few years, I have stabilized this part of the planet, banning infighting that is without cause between Braxian tribes. Rakiz's tribe is the second largest after mine, and he, too, appreciates peace.

However, Lafa has long scrambled for more power.

"I want more spies in his territory," I say. "If he is planning to take advantage of the instability caused by the Voildi's attack in some way, he will be made an example of."

I scan the twelve warriors who make up my council. "Anything else?"

They shake their heads and get to their feet as I leave.

As soon as I'm seated in my preferred workspace, the bells announce yet another interruption.

The human female—Beth, I remember—stands in front of me, leaning on crutches, Tazo standing behind her.

"Hi," she says.

"Hello. What do you need?"

She looks uncomfortable, biting her lip briefly before the words leave her mouth in a rush. "I heard that there's another human woman here. I was wondering if I could see her?"

Alexis's face flashes before my eyes, and I clench my teeth. My initial instinct is to refuse, and I barely refrain from ordering this female to leave.

Alexis will learn that her friend is here. And if I don't allow her to see Beth, she will be even angrier with me. I don't want to see rage in those icy eyes when she looks at me. I like it when they soften, lightening with laughter.

"You may see her," I say finally. "But keep in mind that Alexis will stay here. With me."

The words come out all on their own. I'm like a dragon guarding its horde when it comes to Alexis. Already, I am jealous of others who spend time with her, and she has only been here for one day.

"Okay," Beth agrees.

I force myself to let it go. I have more important things to focus on than the small human female currently safe in my kradi. I nod at Tazo, and he gestures to Beth, leading her away.

I attempt to concentrate, but within moments, I'm

grinding my teeth again. What are the human females talking about?

I ignore the voice that tells me I should give Alexis privacy as I stride back out the door, moving toward the qatal's rooms.

I gesture for the guards to be quiet as I approach, and they're silent as I lean close. I designed these rooms with privacy in mind, so the females' voices are a low murmur.

I lean closer as I manage to catch a few words.

"You haven't heard anything about the other two women taken with you?" Alexis asks.

"We were supposed to look for any trace of them when we were in Nexia, but it all went to hell. I didn't keep a good enough eye on the kid—the one traveling with us—and he distracted Zarix. He nearly died, and I was completely focused on getting him back here."

There's a long pause, and Alexis says something I can't catch. But her words reach me as she raises her voice.

"We know they're with the Voildi, which helps us rule out any other Braxian tribes. And we know the Voildi will likely sell them, based on the way they were talking. That means they're going to have to keep them somewhere. We'll find them."

Alexis's voice is confident, her words assured. After our discussion during the midday meal, I knew she was intelligent, but her reasoning reminds me of one of my councillors. A strange sort of pride warms me even as I attempt to ignore the guards who are watching me listen to the females' conversation as if I am *not* the qatai of this tribe.

The females speak some more and then move closer, and I narrow my eyes as the conversation turns to Alexis's new home.

"Wow," Beth says. "You're living the high life here."

Alexis's voice is dripping with disdain. "I am. But it wasn't my first choice, believe me."

She tells her friend about her experience with the Voildi, and I tremble with rage. I just found Alexis, and yet I could have lost her if Rakiz's warriors had not found the females as they were blindly following the Voildi.

"Tell me about Charlie," Beth says.

"She disappeared. We looked everywhere she could have hidden within the area if she was frightened, and we know she wasn't taken with you guys. Nevada, Ellie, and I actually came to this tribe to ask if they'd heard or seen anything."

"What did they say?"

"Well, first, Dexar wouldn't tell us anything until I agreed to stay here with him." Alexis's voice is bitter, and I ignore the shard of guilt buried deep in my chest.

"For how long?"

"A year."

"A year? Are you kidding me? For a piece of information?" Beth's voice is almost a shriek, and I glance at the guards, who are stone-faced as they stare at the wall.

"Yeah," Alexis says. "In Dexar's own words, he's a 'bad man.'"

"No shit. Had they seen her?"

"One of his sentries had. And get this: apparently they're convinced she was taken by a dragon."

"A dragon? Get out of here."

A long silence, and then Beth's voice is low. "Okay. Say she has been taken by a dragon. How do we get her back? Do you think it...ate her?"

"I find it strange that she was the only one who was bleeding heavily and she was the one who was taken. I think her blood lured it, and I think it took her for a meal. But the others aren't so sure. So please ask anyone you find about the dragon."

"I will," Beth says, and then her voice lowers. "Are you seriously going to stay here for a year?"

I lean closer, but the two females are whispering. I clench my teeth until my jaw aches, but their words are too low to catch. As far as I am concerned, this proves that the little human can't be trusted. She clearly has no intention of fulfilling her side of our bargain.

The two females begin to speak about Zarix, and I turn to leave, uninterested in their female frivolities.

"I wish I could come help you find the other women," Alexis says, her voice heavy with longing, and I snap.

It's as if I'm watching from a distance, unable to control my legs as I stride into the room.

Alexis jumps to her feet. "What are you doing here? Don't you have minions to be ordering around?"

I ignore that. For some reason, it seems entirely necessary that I separate these females immediately.

"Zarix is asking for Beth," I say. Zarix will not deny this if asked.

Alexis's eyes are bright even as her voice turns bitter. "What, I'm not allowed to talk to my friends now?"

I glance at Beth, and the female sighs. "I should get back anyway."

Alexis helps her up, handing her the crutches.

"Come back soon," Alexis says, and the females embrace.

Then we're alone, and Alexis turns away as if she is too disgusted to look at me.

Alexis

Dexar is turning out to be a giant dick. For a moment, he looked angrier than I've seen him, and as soon as Beth left, he turned it off like a switch. Now he seems much more relaxed as he prowls the room like a jungle cat.

"Were you listening to my conversation?" I ask.

He glances at me, stopping in his tracks. "I own everything in this tribe. Including your words."

My mouth drops open, and despite myself, I laugh. His eyes instantly heat, and he takes three large steps, suddenly close enough to touch.

I step back, immediately feeling hunted. There's something predatory about the way he looks at me, but if he thinks he can order me around and listen to my conversations, he's about to learn differently.

I give him a look. "I'm going to let that statement go 'cause I'm just a passenger on your train to Crazy Town. But if you're going to lock me away in here, you should know that I'm a high-maintenance pet. And this bitch bites."

Dexar is silent for a moment as he obviously grapples with whatever translation he's receiving from the device in his ear. He must get the gist of what I'm saying, though, because he frowns.

"I don't want you to be unhappy," he says finally, and I narrow my eyes at him, distrustful of this turnaround. He moves even closer and takes my hand. I allow it, and he strokes his thumb over the sensitive skin of my wrist.

He's obviously expecting this change of tactics to actually work for him. It's likely that the twits on the receiving end of that charming grin fall for his act hook, line and sinker.

I almost snort, and it hits me then. This guy may be a king, but he's still just a man. A man who's in love with himself and is used to everyone else being in love with him too.

Oh, you sad, entitled male.

"If you don't want me to be unhappy, how about you let me have a little more freedom? Do you honestly think I could break out of this place?"

I gesture down at my lengthy dress and thin slippers, and Dexar gives me a long look.

"I believe you could do anything you put your mind to."

I almost flush with pleasure at that.

Get it together, Alexis. He's already got your number.

"Okay, let me be honest here," I say, laying most of my cards on the table. "I want three things. First, I want to learn as much as I can about where Ivy and Charlie could be. Second, I want to talk to the people here about your birth problem and why there are so few females. And third, I want to be able to walk around without Tall, Dark, and Grumpy breathing down my neck."

Rowax has got to go. I've left out the thing I want the most—to get back to our ship and examine it. It's not like we can leave until the other women have been found anyway.

"You expect me to believe that you won't attempt to leave this camp?"

"Look, I'm a curious cat. Sue me. Do I want to know how your security works? Sure. But I'm not an idiot. I've got three hots and a cot here. You think I'm gonna give that up to go wander around in the wilderness by myself?"

Dexar frowns, so I spell it out for him.

"I like my rooms, okay? I like the food, and I sure as hell like that bed."

He sends me a wicked smile. "My bed is bigger."

I run my eyes over his massive body, attempting not to think lustful thoughts. "I bet it is."

His eyes darken, and I clear my throat as the air around us seems to crackle. "So," I say, my voice hoarse. "Are we going to compromise?"

"Compromise." He tastes the word, and I almost laugh.

"A difficult concept for you, I know."

This whole asking for permission thing is more than a little irritating. But one thing I know well is that we have to play with the hand we've been dealt. If sweet-talking the qatai will get me what I want, then that's what I'll do.

"You may have access to the food kradi and all common areas of the camp," he says finally. "You may not go near the training arena, the weapons kradi, the mishua, or the camp walls."

I frown at him as I let that sink in. "The camp walls, the mishua, and the weapons kradi I understand. What's the deal with the training arena?"

He frowns at me. "You are mine. You don't need to be spending time near my warriors."

"There are so many things wrong with that statement that I don't even know where to start."

He shows me the edge of his teeth. "Those are my terms."

"Fine, Your Majesty. I'll stay away from the training arena."

CHAPTER FIVE

D^{exar}

It has been eight nights since Zarix left for Tecar's tribe, taking the boy and the human female with him. Just hours after they departed, Tazo followed them, two more warriors with him.

As soon as they arrived at Tecar's camp, it became evident that Tecar would need hundreds, if not thousands, more warriors than he had available. Not only has Lafa been talking with the Voildi, but he is planning to attack Tecar's tribe and split their territory with Killis, the Voildi leader.

I sent thousands of my best warriors, who marched to Tecar's tribe. I also sent messengers to Rakiz and the other tribe kings in the area with the hope that they will join the battle.

Now there is nothing left to do but wait.

In the meantime, Alexis wanders the camp, speaking to

my people. My warriors watch her, reporting back, but so far she has kept her end of the bargain.

With the battle against the Voildi and now Lafa's tribe, it has been days since I spoke to Alexis myself. I should be content simply to have her in my kradi, yet I find myself missing her smart mouth, husky laugh, and mischievous grin.

Today I will make time to eat with her.

"Qatai?"

I look up as the room goes quiet. Brix has appeared, his eyes hard, and my councillors give him their attention.

"What is it?" I ask.

"A message from Zarix."

"Tell me."

"Lafa is dead. The Voildi leader, Killis, is also dead. One of our warriors was a traitor. His name was Perik, and he was killed. Our forces defended Tecar's tribe, and any Voildi or Braxians who did not die retreated like the cowards they are."

The room is silent. "And Varic?"

"Zarix didn't see him. We believe he survived."

I grit my teeth. Once, news of the warrior's survival would have been met with joy. Unfortunately, the years have changed him. I never expected him to leave my tribe three revolutions ago, and if he decided to follow Lafa and join with the Voildi, he is now an enemy.

We were friends as children. And yet, even after he abandoned my tribe, he never told us of Lafa's plans.

Obviously he is not the same male I once knew.

"Find out anything you can about him." I get to my feet, disgusted. "I will have my midday meal alone."

Not alone. I will finally eat with Alexis again. But these males don't need to know this.

I stride back to my quarters and call for a servant. "Tell Alexis that she will join me for the midday meal."

The servant nods, and within a few moments, they are laying food on the table. Alexis appears, and I drink in the sight of her.

She frowns at me. "You know, you can't just snap your fingers and get what you want all the time."

"I can't?" I smile at her.

"You think you're charming, but you're really just bossy," she says sternly, although a hint of a smile plays around her lips.

"Eat with me, Alexis. I have been busy these days, and I miss the sight of your face."

She hesitates, raising her brow, and I almost smile. Any other female would blush and stutter if I said such words to them. This female is narrowing her eyes at me suspiciously.

Is it any wonder I find myself fascinated by her?

"Why are you so busy?" she asks.

"Eat with me and I'll tell you."

She shrugs, the movement nonchalant, and I have a feeling that she is somehow mocking me. She moves to the table, and I square my shoulders. Unlike our last meal together, this one will not end with harsh words.

She takes a seat, reaching for a cup of water. "So?"

I join her, heaping food onto her plate. It is unusual for a qatai to serve others, but I find myself soothed by the action of giving this female food and watching her enjoy it.

"As you know, Zarix and your human friend traveled to Tecar's tribe."

"Beth. Her name is Beth. Which I'm sure you know."

I eye the female, irritation rising. "Do you wish to fight?"

"No. I wish you to use the name of the woman who

dragged one of your wounded warriors onto a mishua and found help so he didn't die."

I push down the urge to snap at her. Instead, I consider her words.

"You are right," I say, and it's worth the concession to see the surprised pleasure in her eyes. "I apologize."

She rewards me with a smile. "Maybe an old dog can learn new tricks after all."

I don't know what this means, but I nod anyway.

She takes a bite of her food and hums in obvious pleasure as she swallows. "You were saying?"

"Zarix and *Beth* traveled to Tecar's tribe, and there was a battle."

Alexis pauses, leaning back in her seat. "Are they okay?"

"Yes. They killed the Voildi who thought to take Tecar's tribe along with Lafa—the traitorous tribe king who worked with him."

"Awesome. So what happens now?"

"Now my warriors return to camp and we strategize. Any Braxian warriors who joined with Lafa must swear allegiance to new tribes or meet their deaths."

"Deaths?" Alexis's face is pale.

"Betrayal is not tolerated. Those warriors may have sworn allegiance to Lafa, but they knew better than to follow him into battle beside the Voildi. They are lucky to have a second chance."

Alexis pushes her plate away. "So Zarix and Beth will return to this camp?"

I frown. "Zarix is one of my warriors. I do not know what he will do with the—Beth," I finish as Alexis's eyes narrow warningly.

She smirks at me. "You think he'll leave her? You know they're a thing, right?"

"A thing?"

"Yeah, they're together."

I laugh. The idea is preposterous. Alexis's face is serious, and I shake my head.

"Zarix will never take a mate. His life's work has been hunting the Voildi and making them pay."

"A mate?"

I forget that these human females do not know the ways of our people. "One female to sleep next to for the rest of his life. To protect and have children with."

"Oh. Like a wife."

I shrug. I don't know this word.

"You honestly think Zarix is just going to ditch Beth now?"

"I do not spend time thinking about the females my warriors are tumbling."

"You can be a real jackass, you know that?"

"Be careful, female."

"Female? There's just no hope for you. None at all." She shakes her head, and I grind my teeth. Once again, our conversation has devolved to harsh words. Frustration makes my hands clench. Perhaps this is pointless. Perhaps I will never be able to understand this female.

"You are not happy unless you are pushing me." My words are a frustrated growl.

"Well, we can solve that problem. Let me go."

"Never."

Her eyes widen, and I curse myself, backtracking. "You promised to stay for one revolution."

She sighs, and then a strange look comes over her face, and I narrow my eyes.

"You know what?" she says, tilting her head. "Let's make a bet."

"A bet?"

"Yeah. I bet you that Zarix will take Beth as a mate."

I laugh. The idea is ludicrous. "Zarix may have felt responsible for her, may have saved her from one of the Voildi's traps, but that does not mean anything other than he is an honorable male."

Alexis smiles. "Then you won't mind betting on the outcome."

"And what is it you're hoping to receive if you win? Jewels? Credits?"

She laughs. "No. If I'm right, and Zarix takes Beth as his...mate, I get one favor to use anytime I like."

"A favor?"

"Yes. You'll give me something I want."

"And I will receive the same from you," I say, pleased with this idea. I let my gaze travel over her body, lingering on the soft curves of her breasts and hips.

She scowls at me, crossing her arms, and a tiny flicker of uncertainty dances over her face. Then she seems to come to some decision, firmly nodding her head. "Deal."

"A favor," I say. "Be prepared to give me something I want very much, Alexis."

She raises one eyebrow. "Same goes, Your Bossiness."

***

Alexis

"Here are your shoes," Nara says, and I smile at her. She smiles back. Maybe she's finally warming up to me.

We're in my rooms, and I'm getting ready for the day. As much as I've insisted that I can get dressed alone, I have to admit that it's nice to not have to think about what I'm wearing each day.

"Will you eat with the qatai today?" Yari asks.

I pull on my shoes and shake my head, sharing another smile with Nara. Yari is more than a little obsessed with making sure I'm dressed appropriately for the qatai. At first, I assumed Dexar was a hard-ass who actually cared about how much gold thread was sewn into my dresses, but I've never once seen him examine my clothes. If anything, his dark gaze seems to look *through* my dresses.

I wouldn't be surprised if he has X-ray vision at this point.

"Nope," I reply. "I'm going to spend my day annoying the people in this camp."

Yari tilts her head, confused, and I clarify, "I'm going to be here for a few weeks, so I thought I could collate some data for you guys. You know, maybe write a timeline detailing when people began to notice fewer female babies being born and a list of environmental changes."

Yari nods slowly, raising her eyebrows. "You believe you can solve this problem?"

"No," I say. "I'm not that kind of scientist. But I *am* good at collecting data, and at the very least, it'll give me something to do while I'm here. Do you think you could help me find something to write with so I can keep track?"

Yari gestures for me to turn in my chair and begins brushing out my hair.

"Nara will ask the qatai," she says, gesturing toward her, and Nara nods, turning to leave. "Such things are unusual for a female to do," Yari says.

I sit silently while she arranges my hair in some complicated style and we wait for Nara to return. After I called out

Dexar for his inherent misogyny yesterday, we seemed to come to an uneasy truce.

I'm picking over my breakfast when Nara returns, a piece of paper rolled up in her hand. Nara has a blush on her face, and her eyes are sparkling. Perhaps Dexar was in a flirty mood this morning.

The thought doesn't sit well with me, but I'm cheered up as Nara hands me a fat writing implement. I study it, grinning. It's almost like a pencil. I'm not sure what the material is—it doesn't seem as soft as charcoal when I make a tiny line on the paper—but it's definitely not lead.

Whatever it is, I can now write. I thank Nara and Yari and leave my rooms. It's not until I'm standing in the long hall, surrounded by ruby-colored walls, that I remember I have no idea how to get out of here.

I glance at Rowax, who carefully ignores me. No help there. Tavis meets my gaze, and I grin at him.

"Would you show me how to get outside?"

He glances at Rowax, who nods, and I follow him out of the kradi.

"Don't you get bored standing outside my door all day?"

"No, qa-Alexis," he stutters in a rush. "It is an honor to guard one so close to the qatai."

I frown at him. "You realize I'm just a short-term guest here, right?"

He nods, glancing away and reaching for one of the hidden doors. He gestures for me to go through, and I blink as I'm suddenly outside.

"Was this a different route than usual?"

Tavis blushes. "We have been instructed to choose different exits each time you leave."

I grind my teeth. Another little gift from Dexar. That's

enough to make me want to get real good at directions just to spite him.

"Can I ask you a couple of questions?" I ask.

"Of course."

"When did you begin to notice that fewer females were being born here?"

Tavis blushes again at my regard, his gaze flicking away.

"I did not grow up in this tribe," he says. "I chose this tribe a few years ago."

"Which tribe did you come from?"

"Lafa's tribe."

I nod, attempting to make a note on the paper. I question him for a few more minutes, but apparently Lafa's tribe was much smaller than this one, and there were just a few girls Tavis's age when he was a kid.

I thank him for his help, and he moves back into the kradi. I stand in place for a moment, the sun on my skin, ignoring the eyes on me as people walk past.

Sweet, sweet freedom.

I've never been shy about talking to people, but for some reason, butterflies are taking up residence in my stomach as I walk through the camp. It's like I'm a bug under a microscope.

"You're just different, Alexis." I mutter. "Imagine if an alien arrived on Earth."

That thought bolsters me, and I head to the healers' kradi. It's likely that anyone responsible for the health and well-being of the people here will have the most information about the decline in female births.

"Hi," I say as I walk in, and multiple women bow their heads. Okay, this is a little ridiculous. Maybe this is Dexar's way of fucking with me, since he doesn't love the idea of letting me roam free. He's decided to make my life full of one awkward interaction after another.

"Can I help you?" a woman asks, stepping close. She has long dark hair, and her eyes are kind as she smiles at me.

There are at least ten beds in this large kradi, spaced a few feet apart. In the far corner of the room, a woman sleeps on one of the beds while an older woman places the back of her hand against her forehead, likely checking for fever.

Another woman is in the opposite corner of the room, standing in front of a large table. She crushes some kind of herbs, the sweet smell reminding me of cut grass.

I lower my voice. "I was wondering if one of you would have time to answer a few of my questions. It doesn't have to be right now," I say quickly. "Just whenever you have a few spare moments."

The woman glances at the other two healers, and they both nod. She wipes her hands on a cloth and gestures toward a small room I didn't notice at the back of the kradi.

"Why don't we speak privately?" she says.

All righty then. I follow her through the doorway and blink. There must be thousands of wooden containers in here, all stacked neatly on the huge shelves that line the walls. One corner holds a small forest of plants growing in wooden pots. In the center, another worktable sits next to a few wooden stools.

The woman gestures to one of the stools, and I take a seat.

"My name is Elliz," she says.

"I'm Alexis."

She smiles and then sits back. This woman has a calm, peaceful air about her, and I feel my shoulders relax.

"I have a few questions about babies," I say, and Elliz nods as if she was expecting this. She gets to her feet and picks up a small knife before walking to the plants in the corner, cutting a bright-red flower, and bringing it to me.

"One petal with your breakfast each day," she says, and I stare at her, confused.

"Um…"

"You would like to prevent conception, correct?"

"Oh, God no. Well, maybe," I say, flushing bright red at the thought of my bet with Dexar. I have no doubt that the qatai will want a roll in the furs in the unlikely event that he wins our little bet. Truthfully, I'm not opposed to it. Okay, I'm more than a little curious about whether he can back up all that arrogance in bed. I'm damn sure that Beth and Zarix will end up mated, but if they don't…

I reach out and take the flower.

The sexual tension between Dexar and me is real. If we both ever shut up and stop arguing long enough to have sex, I have a feeling it will be incredible. But the last thing I need is to arrive back on Earth pregnant with his baby.

"Now that we've got that out of the way," I say, "I'm actually hoping you can give me some information about the decrease in female births on this planet."

Elliz raises her eyebrows, and I almost laugh. An alien coming to her for birth control doesn't faze her, but asking about birth rates is obviously unexpected.

"Of course," she says. "Do you mind if I ask why you want to know?"

"A few reasons. First, I'm nosy. I don't have a lot to do here, and mysteries fascinate me. I've been this way since I was a kid—just can't seem to help myself when it comes to puzzles. Second, I'm not going to be on this planet for long, but I'd like to help out if I can. It's not uncommon for this type of thing to be environmental, so maybe I can help narrow down some of the potential causes for you guys."

Elliz stares at me for a long moment. "Perhaps you are right," she says finally. "Perhaps something has changed on this planet. Many of us have felt that Braxians were simply cursed by the gods. If you believe you could help, I will tell you anything you need to know."

CHAPTER SIX

Alexis

I'm deep in thought as I make my way back to the kradi. My stomach is rumbling, and I realize I've missed lunch.

According to Elliz, her mother was also a healer, and she began noticing fewer female babies born a few years after the birth of her own daughter. Elliz said that this has been a problem for every Braxian tribe on this part of the planet.

But while it's assumed that there are other Braxian tribes elsewhere, across the "colossal water," Elliz shook her head when I asked if she knew of anyone who had crossed it.

"Mishua cannot swim, and the water is deep with no land in sight. There are other races that come to trade in Nexia, but they have huge contraptions that allow them to traverse the water without getting wet."

I'm guessing she's talking about boats. If I could somehow talk to a Braxian from across the sea or lake, I'd be able to understand if this is a planetwide problem or if it's just something impacting the Braxians on this part of Agron.

I blow out a breath of frustration, coming to a stop in front of Dexar's huge kradi, as I mull over what Elliz told me.

I wish I had more information about this planet. I have no idea how big it is, how many continents it has, or even if Agron is part of the same galaxy as Earth.

"Work with the information you have, Alexis," I mutter as I begin to pace.

Elliz's mom first noticed the slowdown in female births around thirty years ago. I need to study the number of females in each generation and attempt to figure out the rate of decrease. It's not going to be hard data by any means, but I'll work with what I have.

I stare down at my notes and then flip over the long piece of paper. I'm also using this opportunity to figure out where Charlie could be. Dexar said that looking for the dragon's lair is suicide. That means he's not going to tell me what he knows even if he has a good idea where it could be.

I can't do much for Ivy. From what Beth said, she's a fighter, and without leaving this camp, I can't figure out where she is. But Elliz said there have long been rumors about where the dragon could make his home. Since I plan to talk to the people in this tribe anyway, I may as well get some idea of where he could be keeping Charlie.

If she's alive.

I feel eyes on me, and I blink, realizing I've been standing in front of the kradi for a while now, staring at the massive structure as if it can tell me everything I need to know. I walk to the side, away from the main entrance, and smile at one of the guards. His name is Maric, and he's a man of few words, giving me a nod and leading me back to my rooms.

Yari is waiting for me. "Would you like something to eat?"

"Sure. Where's Nara?"

A shadow passes over her face, and she turns away, reaching for a plate of food, which must have been recently delivered.

"I don't know what has changed in her mind," she murmurs. "She has been distant for a while now."

"Did something happen?"

Yari sighs, taking a seat. After multiple discussions—and plenty of urging on my part—she's finally agreed to join me for lunch each day, as long as I'm not eating with Dexar.

She pours me some water and sighs again, her expression troubled. "I feel as if I am breaking her confidence by telling you," she says, and I nod.

"No worries. You don't need to say anything."

She shakes her head. "I don't know if she will return to your service. You deserve to know why."

My curiosity is officially stoked. I take a bite of some kind of root vegetable, discovering that it's not my favorite. I eat it anyway, my stomach begging for food.

"Is she okay?"

Yari nods. "She has propositioned the qatai."

I choke, reaching for my cup of water. "She did?"

I think this over, realizing that I shouldn't be as shocked as I am. Nara is a beautiful woman, the white streak in her dark hair drawing the eye, while her porcelain skin and hazel eyes glow with vitality.

"Yes," Yari says, her face turning hard, and I raise an eyebrow.

"Why is this such a big deal?"

Yari frowns at me and opens her mouth, then seems to catch herself. "Nara is not for the qatai. She knows this."

"Why not?"

The day we met, Dexar bragged about all the women he can "tumble" whenever he wants, so why would Nara be any different? I ignore the shard of jealousy that buries itself in my gut at that thought.

Yari waves her hand. "It is too difficult to explain," she says, and I eye her. Yari has very particular ideas about what is appropriate for Dexar and anyone hanging out with him. And she demonstrates those ideas every time she insists on dolling me up in the best gowns and piling my hair on top of my head before I eat with him.

"The problem isn't that she propositioned him. The qatai is used to this from females young and old," she says, smiling as I snort. "The problem is that she dared to raise her voice to him. He made her leave the kradi and think about what she has done, but he will ensure she is punished."

I scowl at that. I raise my voice to Dexar all the time. If he thinks he can punish Nara, then we're going to be having a heated discussion.

Maybe I'll even raise my voice at him. The horror.

"Sounds like he's being a dick," I say.

Yari looks scandalized, her mouth dropping open. I could've lived without seeing the half-chewed food she displays to me.

She clamps her mouth shut and swallows, changing the subject.

"I think I might take a nap," I say. I do some of my best thinking in those few moments before and after a midday nap, and I have a lot to consider.

"Would you like to bathe first?"

I nod. "That would be great, thanks." I'm dusty and sweaty after wandering through the camp.

Yari gets up, moving to one of the guards, and murmurs a few words.

Back in Rakiz's camp, the servants would haul warm water and dump it into a tub. Here, while they don't exactly have indoor plumbing like I knew it on Earth, Dexar's people have found a shortcut. The water is still hauled and heated outside, but then it's sent into this main kradi through wooden pipes. I'm itching to study how the process works, but the water heating takes place close to the weapons kradi, and that's off-limits according to my agreement with Dexar.

For now.

Within a few minutes, the bath begins to fill with water. There are no taps, and instead, Yari periodically checks the level of water before finally returning to murmur to another servant now waiting outside, who ends the flow of water.

It's a convoluted system, but it's the closest thing to running water I've seen since I landed on this planet, and sinking into a warm tub of water is enough to make me sigh in pleasure.

Yari no longer hovers while I'm bathing and instead leaves to deal with the food. I'll likely see her later once I've finished napping, and I study my leg hair, reaching for a tepi rock. I run it along my legs, removing most of the fine hair. It doesn't quite compare to my Venus, but my legs are pretty smooth once I'm done, and I contemplate my feet while I think.

My toenails still have chipped blue nail polish on them, and the sight seems slightly ludicrous here on Agron.

There's a loud thud from the room next door, as if something heavy has hit the ground, and I frown.

"Yari, is that you?"

Something slams down on my head, pushing me under the water, and I inhale, choking. I push my legs against the foot of the tub for leverage and manage to suck in a breath, but my feet slide as another hand joins the first, this one hitting me in the face and forcing me back under the water.

Panic makes my heart race. I claw at the hands, fighting for my life. Someone's trying to drown me in a fucking bathtub, and if I can't get my shit together, they're going to succeed.

I raise my hand, my nails meeting flesh. The hands loosen slightly, and I take my shot, allowing myself to slide further along the bottom of the bath.

My lungs are begging for air, black dots beginning to appear in front of my eyes. I raise my leg in the air and swing it back, hitting whoever is holding me down.

I'm not going out like this.

I make contact, but it's not enough.

Then the pressure is suddenly gone, and I manage to sit up, coughing and choking.

My lungs exhale water, and I stare in shock as Yari, who has blood running down her head, pushes Nara away from me.

Nara is almost possessed, and she slams into the other woman, hitting her in the head where she's already bleeding.

Yari goes down, and Nara turns as I roll out of the tub, landing on my knees as I continue to cough.

"You crazy bitch," I gasp, but Nara's eyes are blank as she moves toward me.

"You can't have him!" she screams. "I'm the chosen one! Me!"

What the hell is she talking about?

Rowax is suddenly there, and Nara fights like a demon as she's dragged away. The huge warrior probably has a hundred pounds of pure muscle on Nara, but she lunges at me, again and again until I hear something crack.

"Don't hurt her," I snap at Rowax, and he gives me a look.

He pulls Nara away, and then I'm crawling to Yari, who groans as I reach her.

"I need a healer!" I scream, still coughing. And then I flinch back as a huge form fills the doorway. Dexar's face is chilling, the fury in his eyes terrifying as he stares at me for one fraught moment. He reaches for a towel, striding forward and wrapping it around me, and I realize I'm still naked and shivering as I stare at him.

"Healers!" he roars, and Tavis appears, Elliz by his side.

"I'm fine," I say as she steps forward. I point to Yari, and Elliz drops to her knees. Another healer enters, and I flinch. I can still hear Nara screaming as she's dragged away.

My lips are numb as I stare at Dexar. "Why?"

He shakes his head, lifting me into his arms as he gets to his feet. "Are you hurt?"

"No."

"Don't lie to me."

"I inhaled some water. I'll be fine."

Dexar turns to the other healer, whose name I haven't caught. "Follow us."

He carries me out of the bathroom and into my bedroom, using the passageway between our rooms. Once we're in his dining room, he seems to relax slightly, and my eyes widen as he walks through room after room until we finally reach his bedroom. He places me on the bed and gestures for the healer.

"My name is Shoni," she says. "How do you feel?"

I'm no longer coughing, but I'm shaking like a leaf. "Cold," I say honestly. "But I'm fine."

Dexar's pacing the room like a caged tiger, and he curses, grabbing a large fur and wrapping it around my shoulders. I burrow deep into it, still attempting to process what just happened.

"Nara just tried to kill me."

Shoni reaches into a large leather bag, which I didn't notice she was carrying.

"You have a scratch on your cheek," she says quietly. "May I treat it?"

I nod, and she slathers some kind of floral-scented salve onto it. It burns for a moment and then goes numb.

Shoni turns to Dexar. "She will be fine. Look out for any sudden difficulty breathing or any change of color. If her skin begins to turn blue, call us immediately."

Dexar nods. "I want you to stay in Alexis's rooms just in case."

"Of course, qatai."

I stare at the wall, still stunned. Dexar kneels in front of me, and I raise an eyebrow, jolted from my shock.

"Tell me what happened," he says.

"I heard something. A thud. I'm guessing that's when Nara hit Yari in the head. She must've gone down like a bag of bricks."

Fury burns in my belly. Yari is a grandmother. Nara could have killed her. "What the fuck was she thinking?" I ask.

Dexar shrugs. "Keep talking."

I scowl at him, my teeth beginning to chatter as my pulse races. "I didn't see it coming," I murmur. "One moment I was thinking about nail polish, and the next I was under the water. Why would she want to hurt me?"

A muscle twitches in Dexar's jaw, and he gets to his feet.

"She said she was the chosen one," I blurt out. "What was she talking about?"

"The ramblings of the insane don't concern me," he says, and I stare at him.

He's lying like a rug. From the look of retribution in his eyes, he knows exactly what she was talking about.

"What will happen to Nara now?" I ask.

"That is not your concern."

"Of course it is."

He tilts his head, and I realize he's genuinely confused. "The punishment for attacking someone under the qatai's protection is death."

I jump to my feet, the thick fur falling from my shoulders as I clutch the thin towel to me.

"You can't kill her," I snap.

Dexar growls, striding forward, and my mouth drops open as he buries his hand in my tangled, damp hair.

"I can do whatever I like," he says silkily. "You would do well to remember that."

There's no sign of the Dexar I occasionally laugh with right now. No sign of the man who teases me, making outlandish comments while he scans my body with heated eyes.

"Okay," I say. "Take it down a notch."

He simply stares at me. "You could have been killed."

"I wasn't," I soothe. I probably need to give this guy a break. He's the biggest control freak I've ever met. No wonder he's struggling with an attack so close to his own rooms. I don't think he'd truly consider having Nara killed, but there's no doubt that he's on the edge right now.

I reach up, and it's like my hand has a mind of its own. I run my fingers over his furrowed brow, attempting to smooth the lines. When that doesn't work, I push my fingers against the corner of his mouth, lifting them in an attempt to cajole a smile from him.

His expression turns calculating, and then his eyes flare as my finger brushes his lower lip.

Before I can blink, his mouth slams down on mine. My mouth drops open in surprise, and he pulls me close, his hard body pressed against mine.

Uh-oh.

His tongue thrusts into my mouth—caressing, taunting —until I open wider, desperate to taste him back. His arm clutches me to him, his hand sliding over my butt as he hauls me even closer. My nipples tighten in anticipation, and I gasp into his mouth.

I tremble against him, and our kiss turns tender, his lips gentle, his mouth tantalizing, teasing. I assumed he was unaffected, that I was just another one of the females he might like to tumble, but I can feel him pressed against me, hard as stone. His huge body shudders, and he buries his hand further in my hair.

What am I doing?

I raise my hands, flattening them against his chest. He growls in displeasure, slowly pulling away, his eyes so dark they appear almost black as he looks down at me.

This is a mistake. When I took that red flower from Elliz in the healers' kradi, I imagined that I could maybe have a quick roll in the furs with Dexar.

Now I know better.

People leave. They break your heart, and you're never the same again. This time, I'll be the one leaving, but I wouldn't be surprised if Dexar moves on to another woman before I can even get back to our ship. The last thing I need in my life is more heartache.

"What are you thinking?" Dexar's voice is rough. He pushes some of my hair behind my ear, and I lean back, needing space. His arms tighten for a moment, and then he lets me go.

I'm immediately cold again.

"I'm thinking that this is a bad idea."

"Why?"

"I was attacked in your territory. You're feeling pissy and like you've got something to prove. Testosterone is probably coursing through your body, urging you to fuck. I suggest you find someone else to scratch your itch."

Dexar's expression is terrible. "I never took you for a coward."

"Name calling. Real mature."

He stares at me for a long moment, and then his eyes lighten with sardonic amusement. "You're scared. That's fine. I will wait for as long as it takes."

I grind my teeth. "You'll be waiting forever."

"Oh no, Lexi. Eventually, you will become tired of pushing me away," he purrs, and my thighs clench at the way he says the shortened version of my name. "But you may believe whatever you wish."

Alexis

I must doze off because it's not until something moves beneath my head that I open my eyes.

The last thing I remember is Dexar ordering me to rest and the feel of the soft fur beneath my back as I lay down on his bed.

I lift my head, finding him staring at the ceiling. His arm

is wrapped around me, and I blush as I realize I'm still naked. He's wearing pants, but his arm tightens warningly as I attempt to move away.

I narrow my eyes at him as he glances at me.

"I thought you were letting me sleep in your bed alone," I say.

"I was. I changed my mind."

I roll my eyes, once again suppressing a smile. With any other man, the arrogant crap that Dexar says would drive me crazy. And half the time, it does. The other half, I find myself weirdly charmed by the sheer imperiousness that drips from his words and the baffled surprise in his eyes when I call him on his bullshit.

"How long did I sleep?"

My head lifts again at his shrug. "Five or six hours."

"Wow." It turns out that narrowly avoiding death by bathtub sure takes it out of a girl. "Is Yari okay?"

"Her head has been treated, and she will stay in the healers' kradi for observation, but she will be fine."

The muscles in the back of my neck relax as I sigh in relief. "I should go back to my room."

"No."

I tense. "I'm giving you the benefit of the doubt because of your control-freakish ways, but you're pushing it."

He glances down at me. "Tell me about what you learned today."

"Are you serious? We're just going to ignore everything that's happened?"

He nods, and I scowl at him.

"First, tell me you haven't had Nara killed."

"Do you doubt my word?" The question is icy.

"No. But I need to hear it anyway."

"The traitor is fine. She is being kept alive for her trial."

Hopefully, Dexar will have cooled off by then.

"I have a favor to ask you," I say.

Dexar grins down at me. "Perhaps I will grant you this favor in exchange for one from you."

I grind my teeth. "Can't you do anything without a bargain?"

He sighs. "Tell me what you have learned, and I will consider your favor."

Fine. "I talked to Elliz today." I blush as I remember our discussion and the bright-red flower I've tucked away in the large trunk that serves as my closet.

"What did you learn?"

"Not much. Yet. But it's not crazy to imagine that something on this planet has changed enough to have an impact on the number of female births. Even on Earth, the environment has been proven to go hand in hand with the ability to conceive *and* the sex of the babies conceived."

I can't help myself, and I stroke one finger along his chest. He tenses, and I remove my finger. No point tempting either of us.

I clear my throat. "I remember reading about a study they did in Japan that linked warmer temperatures and a lower ratio of male babies born. It turns out that for humans, conceptions of males are more vulnerable to external stress factors."

I push myself up slightly so I can look at Dexar without craning my neck. He's studying me like I've grown another head, and I smile.

"Guys just can't handle stress the way women can." I wink at him.

"You believe this could be what's happening here?"

I shake my head. "I don't believe anything at this point. All I know is that nine months after a disaster like an earthquake or a nuclear meltdown, the proportion of male babies tends to decline for humans. This is just an example, and it's not really relevant here—you guys have been dealing with the change in birth ratio consistently, and it's not like you've had a natural disaster every decade, right?"

He shakes his head. "I understand what you're saying though. You believe there may be an environmental reason for our decrease in females."

"I do, yeah. Let me know if you think of anything that's changed around here over the past few decades. Any differences in your water source, the food you're eating, or anything that made life come to a standstill."

"This makes sense to me. What is your favor?"

"I noticed that there's a spare kradi close to the healers' kradi. I was wondering if I could use it."

Dexar tenses. "You will sleep in this kradi."

I roll my eyes. "I know. I just want to use it during the day. If I could have the space to arrange my notes—thanks for the extra paper, by the way—and people could approach me, I'd be able to work better."

"Why do you need this?"

"People don't know me. I'm showing up at their kradis, and they're immediately on the defensive. If I let it be known that I'm available to talk whenever I'm in the kradi, they might be more likely to volunteer information. Plus, it's a pain in the ass having to be escorted all the way back in here when I forget my notes or something."

Dexar contemplates this for a long moment. "You will still eat with me when I am free."

"Fine."

"You may have the kradi, then."

I grin. "Thank you."

We're both quiet for a long moment.

I glance back up at him. "Are you going to tell me what's really going on?"

"No."

I grind my teeth. "I'll find out," I promise him.

"I have no doubt that you'll try," he smirks, and I want to smack him for his smug tone. "Go to sleep," he says.

CHAPTER SEVEN

D exar

I stalk into my meeting kradi, my mood foul. My councillors wait for me, voices low. By now, the entire camp will have heard what has happened.

What I *allowed* to happen.

When Nara approached me, I was unsurprised. The female has long stuttered around me, usually unable to speak a full sentence. Her mother, Gira, was my mother's close friend, and I am well aware that Gira encouraged Nara to overlook many of the forms of work that Nara was more suited for in exchange for one that allowed her daughter to be close to me.

I found this amusing.

I grind my teeth. If I had not been so quick to dismiss the rumors of Gira's increasing instability and the lies she fed to her daughter, I would never have placed her close to Alexis.

Even when Nara screamed at me, pulling at the white in her hair and pointing toward her eyes, I simply growled at her to leave.

Alexis's brush with death is *my* fault.

I take my seat, and everyone sits down. I gaze at my councillors, but I'm already itching to return to Alexis. The sight of her curled up beneath the furs in my bed felt so right that it took all my willpower to leave the room.

"What do you know?" I ask.

"Our spies report that Varic gathered any remaining warriors from Lafa's tribe. It appears that he has become the new qatai," Andon says.

A headache begins to throb in my right temple. "How many warriors survived?"

"More than we had expected, qatai. A number of warriors from Lafa's tribe chose not to join with the Voildi. Instead, they left the tribe completely. Once Lafa was dead, they chose to return to their tribe under Varic's rule. He swore he would never work with the Voildi, and since so many of them are dead, he is unlikely to go back on his word."

So Varic has finally become a qatai. Just as he always wanted to be.

"Where is he?"

Andon frowns. "That is the problem. We don't know. He found one of our spies and killed him, leaving the body to be discovered. Then the tribe just disappeared."

Orcan snorts. "What do you mean, it disappeared?"

"It vanished. Within a few hours, the entire tribe moved with no sign of where they have gone," Andon says.

"This will allow him to increase his forces," I growl. "I know exactly how Varic will work. Next, he will find other tribe leaders—those with small tribes that have refused to trade with us, or those we have not chosen to trade with. He will attempt to convince them to join him."

"I will make a list of these tribes, qatai," a councilor named Tagar says.

I nod. "Once we have that list, I want those tribes watched for any sign of Varic or his warriors. Is there anything else?"

"Rakiz sent a messenger to report that he is on his way. He would like to speak about potential strategies in person before he returns to his tribe," Orcan says.

"Good. Ensure we are prepared to host him, his queen, and any warriors he brings with him."

Brix is waiting for me outside when I leave the kradi.

"Walk with me," I say, and we move toward the mishua pen. "What did she do this morning?"

"She went back to her rooms. Then she went to the healers' kradi to see the servant. She's still there, talking to one of the healers."

"I want her watched closely. Nara may not be the only one who is a threat to her."

Brix is silent for a long moment, and I glance at him.

"What?" I growl.

"When will you tell her?"

"I won't." If I tell the stubborn female exactly why she is here, she will attempt to leave me. And after listening to the way her incredible mind works, I would not be surprised if she were successful in that attempt.

"With all due respect, this is a risky move," Brix says.

I glance at him. "No one will disobey me."

He shakes his head. "If she finds out..."

I tense, turning to look at him. "This is the only choice that makes sense. For now."

Brix shakes his head. "You are making a mistake."

I growl, watching Alexis appear in the distance as she leaves the healers' kradi. "I have no other option."

Alexis

"Wow." Nevada lets out a low whistle. "This is a bougie-ass life you're living. Good call on taking Dexar's deal."

I grin. "It's so good to see you. How are Ellie and Vivian? Have you seen Beth?"

"I haven't been close to Ellie or Vivian for a while," she says, and I feel my face fall. "Relax, Eeyore. I'd know if they weren't okay. I've been away from camp, kicking ass and taking names."

I reach out and pull Nevada toward the cushions on the floor of my living room. "Tell me everything."

Nevada places her sword on the ground next to her. "I saw Beth. She was with Zarix at Tecar's camp. Turns out that girl is a crack shot with a crossbow. I never would've thought. It's always the quiet ones," she murmurs, her mind clearly elsewhere. She shakes her head. "We're on our way back to our camp, but Rakiz wanted to stop in here and talk strategy and alliances with Dexar."

"You want something to eat?" I wave my hand at some cold cuts, which Yari placed on the table right before Nevada arrived. Nevada takes one look at the meat and her face turns green.

I feel my eyes widen. "Are you—"

"Pregnant? Yup, one-hundred-percent knocked up."

I stare at her while this sinks in. "So I take it our trip home to Earth is down one ass-kicker."

"Yeah, you guys will have to go on without me. But I'm

still going to do everything I can to help you get home. It's just that I'm all loved up with my sugar muffin right now."

I stare at her some more, and she bursts out laughing. "I know. Crazy, huh? The last time you saw me, I was ready to stick Rakiz's head on a pike. But he helped me find Zoey, and one thing led to another. He fought *beside* me, and then, when it looked like there was no way we'd be able to stay together, he tried to give up his title for me. Can you believe that shit?"

I...can. Rakiz and Nevada were like oil and gasoline, their sexual tension thick enough that most people at camp noticed.

"How are you doing?" she asks. "Is Dexar treating you well?"

"I'm okay. Well, I'm okay now. Yesterday was crazy."

I fill her in on what happened with Nara, and within moments, Nevada is up and pacing, a glower on her face.

"I don't get it. What was she talking about?"

"She was screaming. She said she was the 'chosen one.'"

"Oh wow. Full-blown crazy, then. Where is she now?"

"Dexar has her stashed somewhere. I made him promise he wouldn't kill her. She's obviously not okay mentally."

Nevada sighs, slumping back down to the floor. "I'm sorry, Alexis. That must've been awful."

"It wasn't my favorite thing. Dexar just about lost his mind."

"He did, did he? Has he explained why he insists you stay here?"

"Nope."

"Hmm."

"What happened with Zarix and Beth?"

Nevada gives me a look that says she caught the change of subject and she's allowing it. "Oh, they're as loved up as loved up gets. What's that evil smirk on your face for?"

"I have a bet with Dexar. If Zarix and Beth mate, he has to give me something I want. Within reason. And no, he says he won't let me go."

Nevada's face falls, but then her expression turns crafty once again. "Make sure you phrase that favor carefully. I need to hang around camp, and I can't go looking for Ivy or Charlie. Rakiz will barely let me lift my sword now." She rolls her eyes, but it's clear that she's delighted to be pregnant.

"Have you heard anything about Ivy?"

Nevada nods. "She managed to escape, so I'd say it's only a matter of time before we can get a message to her or she's spotted by one of our allies."

My shoulders slump in relief. "That's such good news. So now our biggest focus is Charlie."

I stand and move to my trunk before pulling out the long piece of paper I've been writing notes on.

"What's this?" Nevada asks.

"This is everything I know about the dragon's territory right now. Do you have anything to add?"

Nevada scans the paper, taking my pencil and adding a few notes here and there. Then she glances around, glowering toward the door where the guards are located, and gestures for me to follow her into the bathroom.

She reaches into her pocket and unfolds a piece of paper. "This is the map I created before I snuck out of our tribe. Ignore this part—that's where we found Zoey. I met a guy in the market in Nexia who sells dragon scales. We were able to convince him to tell us the main places where he usually finds the scales, as long as we swore we wouldn't sell them ourselves."

"And?"

Nevada grins. She takes my notes and compares them to the tiny triangles she's placed on the right side of her map. "These are all places where the scales have been found. If we add the information you have, this is what we get."

I stare at the map. Nevada has highlighted Rakiz's, Dexar's, and Tecar's tribes. She's also circled the Seinex Forest and the spot where the Braxians rescued us from the Voildi when we first arrived. The dragon had to have been close enough to that part of the forest to swoop in and take Charlie, but given the spots where his scales have been found, it's clear that he could only have come from one direction.

I hold up the map. "Can I keep this?"

Nevada nods. "It's yours. So what's your plan? You gonna sneak out of here or what?"

I scowl at the reminder of Dexar's unreasonableness. "I'm heavily guarded, like the prized jewel I am," I say, and Nevada laughs. "And unlike you, I can't be trusted with a sword and I have no other weapons. My best bet is to somehow convince Dexar to check out this area. And I know just how I'm going to do it."

CHAPTER EIGHT

D exar

Rakiz is relaxed, his legs stretched out in front of him as one of my servants brings him a cup of noptri. He nods at her before turning his attention back to me as soon as she has gone.

"One of my men has just informed me that Varic is fixated on the human females."

I grind my teeth. "How does he know about them?"

"I didn't see him on the battlefield, but he would have learned about Nevada and Beth. Warriors talk, and by now, he will know about Alexis. You know what this means."

I nod, my mind whirring with this data. If he is searching for human females, it's because Lafa told him why they're so important.

"It's a shame Lafa is already dead. I find myself wishing I could make him suffer."

Rakiz nods. "Eventually, Varic would have assassinated

him. From the way he has managed to win the loyalty of so many warriors so quickly, there's no doubt that he has been attempting to sway them to his side for many months."

"If Varic is looking for the human females, we must find them before he can use them."

Rakiz nods. "I have made a bargain with Vrex at Nevada's insistence." The male's mouth twists wryly, and I raise an eyebrow.

"The rumors are true. Your female has you wrapped firmly around her little finger."

Rakiz bares his teeth in a happy yet feral grin. "I would not have it any other way, my friend."

I tamp down my envy at his obvious joy with his human female. "Vrex will search for the other females?"

"Our agreement covers Ivy—the female with the flame-colored hair who managed to escape the Voildi."

I think on this. Vrex is a good choice. The warrior is larger than most and particularly dangerous. It's rare that a warrior will have no true tribe but will instead make his life removed from any family or community.

While Vrex was born into my tribe, he left while my father was still qatai. There are many rumors about the reason for his choice, but when asked, the warrior refuses to explain why he lives alone.

Vrex is a tool that is used when a task needs to be completed without any chance of failure. His price is steep —a favor he can call at any time. Every tribe king I know owes Vrex a favor—to be called in whenever Vrex feels the need. Many of these kings live in fear of the warrior wanting something that they will not want to give.

Three years ago, a tribe king named Ulix used Vrex to kill an enemy who had blocked one of his key trading routes. The task was complete, and Vrex returned home.

Unfortunately, Ulix could not stand to be in Vrex's debt. He became more and more paranoid about what the other warrior could possibly want when he eventually called in his favor. Ulix was consumed and became convinced that Vrex would take his firstborn child.

Ulix sent twenty warriors to kill Vrex. Vrex sent back twenty heads. When Ulix's tribe learned that he had lost his honor, choosing to kill the other male rather than keep his end of the bargain, the tribe king was assassinated.

"Do you ever wonder what Vrex wants with so many favors?" I ask.

Rakiz shrugs. "I rarely think about that which I cannot control. That way lies madness."

"Do you believe the other human female is still alive?"

"Charlie? I do not see how this could be. Dragix has killed any who approached since before our fathers ruled their tribes. I find it difficult to believe that he kept the human female alive. Perhaps he was simply hungry. However, Nevada wishes for me to investigate this further, so this is what I will do."

"If Dragix does have the female, she is safe with him. The beast would never allow his prize to be taken."

We finish our conversation, and I get to my feet. Alexis should still be sleeping, but I have asked Yari to tell her to meet me in the Great Room.

It took all my willpower to leave her sleeping. If I could, I would ensure she were with me at all times until I lost the sick feeling in my gut. The sick feeling that appeared when I found her naked and shaking on the floor of her bathing room, a deep scratch down one cheek, her eyes blank with shock.

"Safe travels back to your tribe," I say, and Rakiz nods.

"I will let you know if I hear anything else about Varic's location or possible plans."

I make my way to the Great Room and find Alexis waiting. The room is empty and will remain so until I allow my subjects to approach.

Alexis blushes, glancing away, and triumph sweeps through me. My beautiful female is still thinking about our kiss.

My body burns at the thought, my hands itching to pull her close once again. That kiss was born out of a desperate need to see for myself that she was unharmed. Yet I soon discovered that kissing Alexis was unlike kissing any other female I have ever kissed. All thoughts fled my mind, my body shaking with a desperate need to roll her beneath me and make her mine.

"What am I doing here?" She shifts on her feet, still refusing to look at me.

I smile. I have a feeling that it is not a nice smile because her eyes widen when she glances at me before her gaze darts away.

I am a patient male. I will wait as long as it takes for Alexis to admit that she is mine.

"I prefer for you to stay close," I say, and she tilts her head.

"Why?"

"Because that is what I want."

A roll of those icy blue eyes. A sigh and a scathing look. I fold my arms. Alexis may be annoyed at the loss of her freedom, but one thing became evident with Nara's attack. Only I can guarantee her safety.

"Lucky for you, I'm feeling curious and I want to see what happens in this room," she says.

I laugh and gesture to a guard, who picks up a chair,

moving it close to my throne. Alexis sprawls in the chair, her long legs stretched out over one of the arms as she raises her eyebrow.

Once again, I am sure she is somehow mocking me, and the insolent expression on her face makes me long to kiss her again.

My subjects begin to file in, most of them staring at Alexis. She ignores the attention, making notes on the long scroll she carries with her everywhere. I haven't missed the fact that she is now also carrying what appears to be a map, written in her strange language.

I expect that I have Nevada to thank for that.

I sit in my throne, and Alexis looks up.

"So what exactly is happening here today?" she asks.

"Tribe members come to me with petitions and problems that they are unable to resolve themselves. I also choose punishments for those who have broken tribe law and give blessings to my warriors when they take a mate."

"Huh."

I don't know what to make of that, so I lift my hand, and the huge room goes silent as Brix approaches.

"Dispute between two families," he tells me. "Tevar swears that Inax promised that his daughter would mate with his son. Inax disagrees with this."

I sigh. So it begins.

Alexis

I thought I'd use this time to go over my notes—both the notes I've collected about the dragon and the data I'm collating about the female birth rates.

Instead, I immediately get sucked in to watching Dexar rule. He heaves a long-suffering sigh, and I fight back a smile. While it's evident that he'd rather be almost anywhere else, the qatai doesn't hurry anyone who approaches him, taking the time to examine each person's problem from all angles.

First, he deals with two warriors who were close friends, both with an understanding that the first warrior's daughter would mate with the second warrior's son when they came of age.

Unfortunately, the daughter fell in love with a hunter who is rarely at camp, and the son fell in love with a woman from Rakiz's tribe. Neither of them plan to mate with each other, and their parents are still getting used to the idea.

"Sadly, we cannot control the actions of our children, no matter how much we would like to," Dexar says. "I suggest you accept this because this tribe will never be one that takes part in forced matings."

Both warriors bluster, protesting that this isn't what they were asking for. Dexar simply raises one eyebrow. If he were wearing a watch, I have no doubt that he would pointedly glance at it.

Next is a couple who are planning to be mated and looking for their qatai's blessing. The male is wearing gold bands, similar to the ones I spotted around Nevada's wrists. Dexar smiles, leaving his throne to hug the woman and slap her future mate on the back.

Then comes a woman who stands in front of the crowd, her face pale, while I shift uncomfortably in my chair. She's pretty, with a restrained kind of beauty that makes you take a second look.

"Let me understand, Parit," Dexar says. "You would like me to order a warrior to be your mate?"

Parit flushes, and I shoot Dexar a look. There's no need to be mean.

"He promised me," she says quietly. "It has been understood that we would mate since we both learned what mating truly means."

Aw. Poor thing. Her guy has done her dirty, but instead of moving on with her life, she seems to think her qatai will step in.

Even I know better.

"And you believe I should order him not to mate with the female he has already pledged himself to?"

She hesitates but nods, and I sigh. Whispers break out amongst the crowd, and Dexar raises his head, green eyes scanning his subjects. Within moments, the room is silent.

"You know better than this," Dexar says gently, and her eyes fill with tears. "You know I will not order anyone to mate against their will in this tribe."

She does know. It's clear by the jut of her chin that this was what she was expecting to hear. This wasn't about attempting to force this guy to be her mate. It was about telling everyone—including the qatai—about what he had done.

One thing I've learned on Agron? For Braxian warriors, honor is everything. And this woman has just painted herself as a victim, ensuring that everyone will look at her with pity, while her ex-boyfriend will be seen as a two-timing asshole.

Dexar glances at me. "What do you think the solution is to this problem?"

More whispering. I feel my face heat and send him a killing look. A smile plays around his mouth, and I want nothing more than to sucker punch him for drawing more attention to me.

"I have no idea. I'm not the ruler here. You are."

Dexar's smile widens. "And what would you say to this woman if you *were* the ruler?"

"You want to give me your job?"

He simply gestures to Parit, who looks uncertain.

I sigh. "If I were the ruler here, I would encourage you to move on with your life," I tell her honestly. "By coming here and painting yourself as the victim, you've made yourself look weak. Is that what you were hoping to achieve?"

The room is so silent it's as if no one is even breathing.

"No, qatal."

I frown at the word and glance at Dexar. The smile has left his face as he narrows his eyes on the woman. The color drains from her face, and she takes a deep breath.

"He passed me over," she says suddenly. "He made me promises, and then he chose another female. He lied to me."

Gasps sound. Parit is determined to paint her ex as a man without honor.

"Did he choose this woman while you were still together?"

"I don't understand."

"Alexis is asking if this male was still visiting your furs while also visiting those of another."

Her face burns bright red, but I have little sympathy. She chose to air her dirty laundry in public. Now she gets to deal with the consequences.

"No, qatai."

I tilt my head. "So he told you that he no longer wanted to be with you *before* he turned to another woman?"

Parit has tears in her eyes when she looks at me, but she nods her head.

"That's called life," I tell her. "Sometimes, no matter how hard you try, things just don't go your way."

Tears are rolling down her face now, and I sigh. It's not that I don't have any sympathy for this woman; it's just that I hate seeing how she's burning her own life to the ground in an effort to throw shade at her ex.

If there's one thing I've learned in this tribe, it's that the people here gossip about everything. Instead of choosing to move on and be happy, Parit has turned her life into a spectacle.

Some people just don't have enough grit. They lack resilience. When their world falls apart, they fall apart with it, and they spend so much energy feeling persecuted and victimized by life that they forget to do the most important thing.

Pivot.

I get it, change sucks, especially when you're not used to it. But most people spend so much time fighting change that they forget to search for the opportunities it brings.

"What is your ruling?" Dexar asks me.

"There is no ruling. There's nothing that can be done here. Happiness is the best revenge, so I suggest you move on." I pause, thinking for a moment. "I recently heard that occasionally, the women here will move to other tribes to find their mates. This is completely up to you, of course, but sometimes, a fresh start can be just what you need."

Parit seems to think this over, finally nodding. There's nothing else to say, and she backs away, moving toward the large entranceway.

"What was that?" I mutter to Dexar.

"Just making sure you don't fall asleep over there."

I narrow my eyes at him, and he winks at me. Then his face turns cold as he glances up at the entranceway.

Nara is walking in, a guard on either side of her. She's still wearing the dress she was wearing when she attacked me, and the sleeve has a rust-stained blotch of blood on it. Yari's blood. I swallow back bile.

"What's going on?" I murmur, and Dexar glances at me.

"This is Nara's trial."

"Where's her representation?"

"Excuse me?"

"Who is going to argue her side?"

"There is no side. She attacked you and was caught in the act."

Shit. As much as I hate what Nara did, it's clear that she wasn't in her right mind.

"Fine. I'll represent her."

"No, you won't."

I grind my teeth until my jaw hurts, watching as Nara is led closer until she's just a few feet away.

Dexar's face is cold as he eyes her. "You attacked Yari with no provocation and attempted to kill Alexis—a female under my protection. What do you have to say in your defense?"

This isn't a trial. It's a fucking sentencing. It's difficult to reconcile this man with the guy I see when we're alone.

I wonder if it's even more difficult to never be able to show your true self in public. To have to be seen as a cold, merciless ruler.

"I am the chosen one," Nara says, her eyes pleading as they stare up at Dexar. "Ask my mother. She will tell you."

Dexar's eyes narrow with a hint of pity. It's clear that whatever is going on in Nara's head is likely thanks to her mother.

"Bring Gira forward," Dexar says, and the crowd murmurs as an older woman steps through the entranceway, also escorted by guards. She looks so similar to her daughter that if she had no lines on her face, and if her hair also had a white streak, it would be difficult to tell them apart.

"You know of the crime your daughter has committed. What do you have to say for your lies?" Dexar asks.

"They're not lies," she spits. "I have known since she was a child that Nara was to be the chosen one. Look at her!"

You could hear a pin drop as Dexar gets to his feet. Even I know better than to order Dexar around in public.

"I am looking," Dexar says softly. "And all I see is a female who has been twisted by her mother's falsehoods. You are the true culprit here."

I open my mouth and then slam it closed. Nara's actions are her own, but her mom should also be held accountable for her part.

Gira turns to me, her eyes filled with hate. "You are a pretender!" she shrieks, and I tense as she leaps toward me. The guards are holding her tight, and she doesn't move, but I shiver at the look on her face anyway. If she could, this woman would kill me right now.

I don't understand it. I've been in this tribe for approximately five minutes. What could I have done to inspire such loathing?

"You are nothing but a slut," Gira says. "You will never be the chosen one."

Dexar nods at one of the guards, and he slaps his hand over Gira's mouth.

"So," Dexar says softly, turning to me. "What is the punishment for attempting to murder another on your planet?"

I gulp. "Prison," I croak out. "Those who are *proven* guilty are sent to prison."

Dexar shakes his head. "We do not imprison females on this planet."

"But you put them to death?"

"Neither I nor my father have ever needed to do such a thing." Dexar eyes both women, and they pale. "But there is a first time for everything."

Somehow, I know he's bluffing. Dexar has no intention of putting these women to death, but he's obviously proving a point here so that word will spread about his leniency. He needs to be able to give that mercy without appearing weak. He can't have anyone attempting murder so close to his own rooms.

I clear my throat, suddenly certain that he wants me to play along.

"I'm asking for mercy," I say, and Dexar turns to me, tilting his head.

"What was that?" he purrs, and I narrow my eyes at him.

"Mercy," I say, raising my voice so that everyone in the room can hear.

"These women have committed a grievous crime," he says, and I can see people in the crowd nodding firmly.

"Death," an old woman hisses, and Dexar raises his eyebrow at me.

I wish I had my trump card to play right now. But Zarix and Beth aren't here, so I have no proof that they're planning to mate, which means Dexar's unlikely to give me that favor he'll owe me.

"Death is not something I am comfortable with," I say, choosing my words carefully. "I have done my best to integrate into your culture, but as one of the victims, I am pleading for mercy."

"A bargain," Dexar says, and I squirm as the crowd goes silent again. Bargaining with Dexar never ends well.

"What kind of bargain?"

"You will move into my rooms."

"No!" Nara cries, and a guard slaps his hand over her mouth as well.

I stare at Dexar. Something tells me that I've been played. He lifts his brow, and I wish nothing more than to be alone with the infuriating jackass so I can tell him exactly what I think of this particular bargain.

"Fine," I grind out, and his smile is blinding.

He turns to the two women, his face hardening once more. "You will leave this tribe. You will not be welcome back here, nor will you be welcomed by any of our allies. I suggest you find work in Nexia."

The crowd erupts, and Dexar's eyes stay cold as the two women are led away.

CHAPTER NINE

Alexis

"This is some bullshit right here," I mutter as three overly muscled warriors haul my wooden trunks into Dexar's rooms. The qatai raises his eyebrow from where he's sitting at the table eating breakfast but keeps his eyes on whatever he's reading.

"You made a bargain," he reminds me, and I grit my teeth.

"I like my rooms." Yes, I'm sulking.

Dexar finally raises his head. "You'll like these better. This is for your own safety."

"There's no reason to think that anyone else would hurt me. Nara wasn't in her right mind."

"Regardless, you made the deal. In front of hundreds of witnesses, I might add."

"That was underhanded, by the way. If you wanted me

in here, why'd you have to bargain in front of everyone else? Now they'll think I'm sleeping with you."

I kick out at a padded chair, and Dexar grins.

"You are sleeping with me."

"We may be sharing a bed, but I'm not having sex with you."

"Yet." He pushes back from the table and prowls toward me. "You're not tumbling me *yet*."

I attempt to ignore the way the muscles in my lower stomach clench at the heated look in his eyes. That way lies madness. How can I possibly be so damn charmed by this primitive barbarian?

"You're not as sexy as you think you are," I mumble, and he flashes me a wicked grin, stepping even closer.

The bells ring, announcing a visitor, and Brix appears.

"Zarix has returned, qatai."

My eyes widen. "Is Beth with him?"

Brix nods, his mouth quirking. "A human female has traveled with him, yes."

I grin at Dexar, and he raises his eyebrow. "I'll have Beth sent to you," he says.

"I'm going to go work in the other kradi," I say. "Can you have her meet me there?"

He nods, and I smile at him.

"Thank you."

My thoughts are racing as I make my way to the small kradi I've designated as my office. My map hangs on the wall, and I study it. I have no idea whether Dexar will actually let me travel to the dragon's territory.

He stipulated that the favor could be anything as long as I didn't leave. Technically, this would mean leaving the camp even though I'd be returning.

I chew my lip. Dexar is tricky. I should've been more specific with my wording.

"Hey!"

I turn and jump to my feet, wrapping Beth in a hug. "How are you? How's your leg?"

She glances down at it ruefully. "Well, I'm off the crutches, and I'm slowly strengthening it. I'll never be a professional dancer again, but that's kind of a moot point now."

"It is?"

She smiles. "Yeah. I've decided to stay here. Zarix and I are planning to have a mating ceremony just as soon as we round everyone up. I want everyone to be there together, you know?"

Wow. First Nevada and now Beth. And then there's Ellie all knocked up back at Rakiz's tribe. These girls are dropping like flies.

I grin. "I get it. I'm so happy for you. Not only are you in luuurve, but you've just helped me win a very important bet."

Beth pushes her long dark hair off her shoulder and raises one elegant brow. "Oh yeah?"

We sit cross-legged on the floor while I explain my bet with Dexar, and Beth laughs when I tell her how Dexar insisted Zarix would never take a mate.

"I wouldn't have believed it myself," she says. "The guy was the definition of a dedicated bachelor."

"Beth?"

We both turn as Javir pokes his head in the kradi. His face is blue, his eyes slitted, and he grins at Beth as if she's his best friend.

"Alexis, you remember Javir," Beth says.

"I do."

"He's going to be staying with me and Zarix from now on."

Javir shoots her a look so filled with love that my heart melts.

Then his gaze fixates on the map I've hung on the far wall of my kradi. "Wow," he says. "What are you looking for?"

"Dragons," I say, and he snorts.

"There's only one."

"Yes, so I've heard."

Javir steps closer, studying the map. "This is wrong," he says. "Dragons hate the heat."

"One of his scales was found near that desert."

Javir shrugs. "Maybe he lost it while he was flying over, or maybe he was hunting. Everyone knows Dragix lives in the mountains."

I stare at him. "They do? He does?"

Javir gives me a look like I may be the dumbest adult he's ever met.

"Javir," Beth says warningly, and he rolls his eyes.

"Braxians don't know anything about Dragix. They stay in their tribes and they avoid him because he would eat them up."

"But you know about him?"

"People who live in the forest know about him. We know when not to hunt and when to avoid certain areas."

I stare at the kid. "Tell me everything."

He laughs and sits down cross-legged before leaning forward intently. "Well, Dragix hunts at dawn and dusk. He usually eats animals, but if you're stupid enough to be where he's hunting, he either can't tell the difference or he doesn't care."

I mull over that. "So he eats people?" This is bad news for Charlie.

Javir shrugs. "One time, when my mother was young, a pack of Voildi hunted the dragon." He grins fiercely. "Dragix blew fire and burned them up. Voildi must taste bad because he didn't even eat them. He just dumped the bodies back in Voildi territory." Javir's voice is low with awe. "His fire is so hot some of their bones had turned to ash."

I gulp. The more I learn about this dragon, the more scared I become. "Does he have any weaknesses?"

Javir snorts. "He's a dragon, lady."

I narrow my eyes as Beth makes a warning sound low in her throat, and Javir sighs.

"Some say that he can turn into a man and if you stab him with a nix-tipped spear while he is transformed, he will die. Others say that if you cut off his tail, he will be driven mad with rage."

I mull over that. Nix is similar to gold. The intricate designs on most of my dresses have been made with a mixture of nix and some other metal, which allows it to be woven into a thread.

I blow out a breath. "And you think he lives in those mountains?" I gesture at the map, and Javir nods. It makes sense when I study the map. If the dragon loses his scales when he's flying, or when he lands to hunt, there's a clear pattern that points to the mountains.

"The dragon likes shiny things," Javir says. "Maybe if you took some nix and jewels, you could distract him. That way, he might not kill you as soon as he sees you."

Dexar

"So, Your Majesty, it seems as if you owe me a favor."

I hold back a grin as I raise my eyebrow, taking another bite of my food. As surprised as I was to learn about Zarix's impending mating, I'm more than a little curious about the type of favor Alexis could want.

I swallow. "And what favor could this possibly be?"

Alexis grins, eyeing me over her cup. Earlier, she asked to try my noptri, and the expression on her face after she finished coughing and gagging was enough to make me roar with laughter.

Yari bustles in before refilling our cups, and Alexis waits until she has gone before she sits back in her seat, narrowing her eyes at me.

"I know where the dragon is," she says, suddenly serious. "For my favor, I want to travel to the dragon's territory and see if I can find any signs of Charlie."

My heart pounds in my chest at the thought of her getting close to the dragon.

"That is suicide," I snap, and she tilts her head.

"You've said that before. I don't think it is. From every-thing I've learned, Dragix is capable of critical thought. I don't think he'd kill us without provocation."

"Going anywhere near his lair will be seen as provoca-tion," I growl, getting to my feet.

Alexis simply watches me pace. "I'm not saying I want to walk up to a sleeping dragon and pull its tail. Give me some credit. I simply want to see if there's any sign of Charlie." She sighs. "Look, Dexar, we're all trying to find Ivy and Charlie. When you made that bargain with me, you took me out of the game. These women are counting on us. They want to go home."

"And do you want to go home?"

She's silent, and I grit my teeth.

"You have never told me what is so special about your planet," I say. "Why are you so eager to return? Do you have a lover waiting for you?"

I'm gratified by the look of surprise on her face, but it doesn't help my mood. Last night, Alexis curled up against me, falling straight to sleep. Lying next to the beautiful female without tumbling her was torture of the worst kind, and it took many hours before I could fall asleep.

"No," she says finally. "I don't have a lover waiting for me."

"So what is it? What is so important there?"

She stares at me as if I've suddenly become insane, and I fight back a growl.

"I have friends that I miss and a career that I love."

"What is this 'career'?" There is no translation, and Alexis raises her eyebrow as I attempt the word.

"It means I had a purpose. Something I trained at for many years, that I was paid to do. It made me feel happy and fulfilled."

I wave my hand. "You could have the same on this planet."

She shakes her head, and a look of longing crosses her face. I should not have reminded her of this career. Already, I can see her thinking about it fondly.

"You obviously can't be reasoned with right now," she says. "We can continue this discussion later."

I fight back a snarl as Alexis turns, walking out of the kradi. She leaves her papers on the table, and I fight back the urge to tear them to pieces.

Instead, I follow her.

She glances back at me warily but continues to walk

down the corridors. She has obviously memorized one of the exit routes, and she throws me a triumphant look over her shoulder as she walks out into the sun.

I glower at her as she stalks toward the kradi she now uses for her "research." I have been good to her. I have given her everything she could possibly need in this tribe. And yet she still wants to leave.

"Qatai."

"What?"

Brix looks taken aback by my snarl, and I sigh.

"I apologize. I have had an argument with Alexis. She was attempting to convince me to let her go near Dragix's territory."

Brix's eyes widen, and he turns. We both watch as Alexis approaches her kradi, flicking me one last burning glance over her shoulder.

The ground shakes and heat fills the air as the kradi explodes.

I'm running as flames shoot from the kradi, the air thick with smoke.

I can't see Alexis. I can't see her.

I roar her name, shoving people out of my way.

A guard attempts to stop my approach, and I punch him in the gut, pushing him to the ground.

I catch a glimpse of her long blonde hair, standing out like a lantern. She's alive. She's alive and *crawling into the kradi.*

She must be confused. Brix appears, throwing a water-soaked blanket to me. I catch it and move to Alexis, attempting to wrap it around her.

She coughs. "Stop," she orders.

"You're going the wrong way."

"My map," she chokes out, still fighting me. "Just let me grab my map."

I take the blanket and wrap it around my head, and water soaks me as Brix appears with more guards, all of them attempting to put out the flames with buckets of water.

I lunge into the tent, ignoring the scream that rips from Alexis's throat.

CHAPTER TEN

A lexis

My teeth are still chattering with shock as I sit next to Dexar. He's surrounded by healers, and somehow, he's incredibly, furiously alive.

My map is now clutched in my hand.

I think I was in shock. I definitely wasn't thinking straight, risking my life for a piece of paper. If I'd taken a moment to think, I would've left it, but Dexar jumped into action, running into the kradi as if he were about to save a living, breathing person.

Dexar has burns on his lower legs. He wrapped a blanket around his head and shoulders, and he was wearing shoes. But he leaped through the flames, grabbing the map before using his knife to cut his way out of the opposite side of the kradi.

Dexar groans in pain, and I reach for his hand.

"Why'd you do it?"

He squeezes my hand. "You wanted it."

"I don't understand you."

He shifts, obviously in pain as a healer cuts away the legs of his pants.

"I'm sorry," I whisper, and he meets my eyes.

"You should be," he says bad-temperedly, a growl leaving his throat as one of the healers slathers a particularly nasty-smelling paste on his leg.

I chew my lip, and Dexar sighs, pulling my hand closer. He glances at Elliz, and she tilts her head at the other healers, moving away with them.

"What were *you* thinking?" he asks. "Again, you could've died."

I frown at him. "Trying to go in for the map was a bad call, I'll give you that. But it's not my fault that someone tried to kill me. Oh my God. Someone tried to kill me. Again." I feel the blood drain from my face, and Dexar squeezes my hand.

"I agree," he growls, and the expression on his face is frightening. "You are the only one who uses that kradi, and if you had entered a moment earlier, I have little doubt that you would be dead now."

I lean over and shove my head between my knees, holding back the urge to vomit.

"Why would someone want to kill me?" My voice is muffled, and Dexar takes a moment to reply.

"I will find out," he promises. "My warriors are examining the kradi sand surrounding area and talking to all witnesses. For now, you will stay with me. I mean it, Alexis. No exceptions."

I raise my head. "Okay," I say meekly. If I've got a target on my back, I'm not going to do anything dumb. I'll practically glue myself to Dexar if it means I'm not going to get blown up.

I lean down again and push my head back between my knees.

Elliz's soft voice breaks the tense moment. "The burns are not as bad as they first looked, qatai. This salve will remove the pain and prevent infection, and you should avoid getting the bandages wet. You should also rest for the next few days."

I lift my head again as Dexar nods, releasing my hand as he gets to his feet. I can tell by the mutinous look on his face that he has no intention of resting.

Elliz and I share a long look, and I nod at her.

She smiles. "Are you okay, Alexis?"

The healers have already treated my scrapes and cuts. I was thrown free of the kradi, and it was my own damn fault that I almost singed off my eyebrows trying to get back into it.

I clear my throat. "Actually," I say, "I don't feel very well."

Dexar tenses beside me, his eyes flying to mine, and Elliz nods.

"That's perfectly normal," she says, her face serious, but I can see merriment in her eyes. "It would be a good idea for you to rest too."

I glance around. "I don't want to stay here."

"You may return to your rooms if you like."

I nod, glancing at Dexar from beneath my lashes.

"I will return with you," he says, and I hide a smile. The urge to smile leaves me when he takes a step. His face is blank, but I swear I can *feel* his pain, and my gut twists with guilt.

"I'm really sorry," I say again, and he reaches for my hand, helping me to my feet.

"You can make it up to me," he says with a lecherous grin, and Elliz suddenly goes deaf and blind, busying herself with scooping salve into a wooden jar. Then she reaches for a bottle of liquid.

She hands them both to Dexar but addresses me. "The salve needs to be applied twice a day and the pain tonic taken when needed," she says, and I nod. Dexar narrows his eyes at her, obviously unhappy with this turn of events, and he guides me toward the door.

Guards immediately surround us, and I flinch back.

"Relax, Alexis. They'll escort us back to our rooms."

Brix is silent as the grave as he follows us, and I glance over at where the remains of my kradi lie in the ashes. I was so mad at Dexar this morning that I left my notes on the table. With the map in my hand, I'm only down a few pieces of paper and some scribbled thoughts.

I still can't believe he went in and grabbed that map for me.

Dexar is coolly logical. He has no heir, and if he were to die, his people would have no qatai. And yet he risked his life for me *and* my map.

"Bring me any information you can in the morning," Dexar orders Brix.

Brix nods. "We *will* find out who did this, qatai."

Dexar must be in excruciating pain, but he never limps, just walks slowly and steadily to his rooms. *Our* rooms now.

"To bed," I tell him, and he grins at me, waggling his eyebrows. Finally, he quits the macho act and gives into a wince as he makes his way through his rooms.

He strips off his clothes, and I pull back the blankets, trying my best not to look.

"Since you feel so unwell, you will lie with me," he says, and I flick my gaze to his.

I sigh. "You saw through that, huh?"

I guess it was obvious that Elliz and I were just trying to get him back here to rest.

Dexar gives me a slow nod, and I climb in beside him. He immediately hauls me close.

"Be careful!" I yelp.

"I can no longer feel any pain," he says. "The salve has done its job."

"Well, you were still burned," I mutter. "You need to make sure you don't do any further damage."

Dexar's voice is low and pleased. "Were you worried about me, Lexi?"

I feel my cheeks redden. "Of course I was," I snap.

The dimple appears in his cheek once again, and I stare, fascinated.

Dexar's grin widens. "I know what will make me feel better," he murmurs, his gaze dropping to my mouth.

I blow out a breath. "You're meant to be resting. That means no hanky-panky."

"Kiss me, Lexi," he orders. I sigh, giving in and leaning over him as I push my hair out of the way. He allows me to lead this kiss, and I tease him, brushing over his mouth once, twice, and then nibbling at his lower lip.

"Alexis," he groans roughly.

I smile against his lips, and he buries his hand in my hair, pulling me down as he takes my mouth.

Had I thought he was allowing me to lead? Dexar conquers my mouth, and I moan against him, goose bumps breaking out along my arms. He rolls me on top of him, and I squeak, instinctively straddling him as I fight not to brush my feet against his poor burnt lower legs.

"Dexar," I begin, and he ignores me, deepening our kiss as he positions me where he wants me. He's hard and hot, and my heart races as he pulls me even closer until he's nestled between my thighs. I gasp at the feel of him, tantalizingly close to my pussy.

He breaks our kiss, moving to run his lips along my neck, nipping and stroking. I arch, rubbing against his cock, and he groans out a rough curse.

Obviously, I'm not the only one affected.

"Take your dress off," he murmurs.

"No way," I say, slapping at his hands as he moves to untie my dress. I push back, and he stares at me, his eyes hot, his jaw tight, and one eyebrow raised in an expression that clearly says "you gotta be kidding me."

"Absolutely not," I scowl at him. "You heard the healers. You're supposed to be resting."

He narrows his eyes. "Alexis," he says seriously, "do you want me?"

I flick a glance down to where I'm straddling him. It takes every ounce of my self-control not to grind against him like a hussy.

"You know I do," I say. There's no point denying it.

His eyes flare hotter. "I want you too. What do I have to do to make this happen?" His mouth twists. "You have the qatai of the largest Braxian tribe begging you, female. Is that what you need?"

I scowl at him. "Don't get pissy with me. I don't want the qatai. I want Dexar." His eyes widen slightly, and I continue, biting out the words. "And I don't want our first time to involve you wincing in pain."

He considers this. "What if I let you ride me?"

I laugh. "Oh, would you *allow* me to ride you, Your Majesty? I knew you were the type to not do any of the work in bed."

He grins at me. "I like that you tease me," he says

suddenly, frowning slightly as if surprised. "No one else would dare."

I snort and open my mouth, but he already has his hands beneath my butt, and my mouth drops open as he raises me until I'm positioned over his head.

I turn bright red, and he winks at me. "Remove the dress and ride my face, Lexi."

"Uh..."

"I'll make it good for you," he promises.

I'm not an idiot. I lose the dress.

I'm still wrestling the dress over my head when he pulls me close until I'm straddling his face. Then he feasts on me. I gasp out a curse as he strokes the flat of his tongue along my slit, then uses the point of it to dance mercilessly over my clit. He alternates between stroking and sucking, holding me in place as I grind down, breathless now as I reach for release.

"Please, Dexar," I groan, and he hums against me in approval, the vibration making my thighs shake as I inch closer. My hips rock, and he reaches up, tweaking my nipple just as he sucks firmly at my clit, pushing a finger deep inside me.

I shatter into a million pieces, the pleasure going on and on. I'm gasping, slumped over him, but he wastes no time, pulling me back down until I'm positioned over his cock.

Dexar leans up, his mouth closing on my breast as he plays with my nipple. Just like that, I'm desperate again, and his laugh is low and rough as I moan.

I slide my hands up his chest, running my fingers over the blue-green scales that cover his shoulders and upper arms. They're obviously sensitive because Dexar is no longer laughing, his jaw clenched as his hands tighten where they're clamped on my butt.

His hand slides down, skilled fingers driving my pleasure higher, and I writhe, desperate to feel him inside me. Then he reaches down, and I sigh. *Finally.*

The thick length of him stretches me as he thrusts inside me, and it's his turn to groan as I clench around him. I lean on his chest, my hands keeping me steady as I ride him, lost in pleasure. Dexar stares at me, and I feel suddenly vulnerable. But the awe in his eyes is like a drug, stealing my inhibitions.

I squeeze around him, and he growls. I laugh, suddenly desperate to see this arrogant king lose control.

He narrows his eyes at me, and then he grins, sliding his hand down to where we're joined. My head falls back, and I groan, almost losing my balance as he strokes my clit.

I'm shaking, gasping, my hips moving with quick snaps as he uses his other hand to pull me down, his hips rising as we chase our pleasure together.

I climax, shuddering, my teeth clenched as I squeeze around his length. Dexar pulls me down for one last thrust, emptying himself into me, and I collapse on his chest, panting.

So much for "I will not sleep with the tribe king." *Way to hold out, Alexis.*

Dexar's hand strokes my butt, and I snuggle closer.

"Are your legs okay?"

I feel his head move as he nods. "The salve is potent. And you? I didn't hurt you, did I?"

My muscles are sore, but not from the explosion. As my face heats, I bury it in his chest and shake my head. He laughs.

Time for a change of subject.

"What's it like being the qatai?"

Dexar shrugs, his hand moving up to stroke along my

lower back. "I always knew I would rule. My father was from a small tribe that was conquered by a much larger tribe. He lost both his parents and his siblings that day and almost died himself. He vowed that he would create a tribe that was so big no one would ever think to take it from him."

"And he raised you to think the same way."

It's all making sense now. Why Dexar has grown his tribe to be so large. Nevada once called Dexar obsessive with his need to grow his army.

"Yes. The people in my tribe know that everything I have done, every territory I have claimed, is to make us stronger. My future mate will not have to fear for her life. Will never watch our children be slaughtered by invaders."

Dexar's voice is grim, but I can't help but focus on his words. *His future mate.* I judged Dexar as an arrogant play-boy, but since I've been here, I've seen a side of him that I never expected to see. Sure, he's still arrogant, and I'm sure he's still a playboy, but one day, when he does take a mate, I have no doubt that he'll be loyal to her. He'll protect her and keep her safe, along with any children they have.

I bite my lip. It's a good thing I'm planning to get back to Earth. 'Cause there's no way I could watch him take a mate. My hands clench at the thought.

"Are your parents still alive?"

"My father died in his sleep. My mother is still alive." His voice is warm. "When she hears about what happened today, she will likely march in here and give me a piece of her mind."

Dexar shifts, obviously uncomfortable.

"You need some medication for the pain," I say.

He shakes his head. "Distract me. Tell me things about you. What did you do on your planet?"

I smile. "It's kind of ironic actually. I'm an astronautical engineer. My team focused on spacecraft design. When the Arcav invaded, we were attempting to figure out how their ships worked so we could replicate them. And then I ended up transported by an alien spaceship and sold before crash-landing on this planet."

"This is why you want to get back to your ship."

I nod, and I'm practically holding my breath as he's silent for a long moment. Thankfully, he changes the subject.

"And your parents?"

I clear my throat. "Um. I never knew my parents. I was abandoned on a church doorstep when I was just a few hours old."

"I don't understand."

I shrug, avoiding his gaze. "I was found by a priest and put into foster care. You'd think I would've lucked out—I mean, babies are usually in high demand. But nope."

"Your parents abandoned you?" Dexar's voice is incredulous, and I squirm in embarrassment. It's not often that I tell anyone about my childhood, and I'm not quite sure why I've decided that now is the time to tell Dexar. It's difficult enough to tell a fellow human how I was left in a cardboard box, wrapped in a towel. But on this planet, children are precious and family is everything. How can Dexar possibly understand?

I swallow around the lump in my throat.

"I don't know if it was a joint decision or if my mother was a scared teenage girl who was hiding a pregnancy. I don't know if she was forced to give her baby up or if she simply couldn't deal with it. Either way, no one wanted me."

Dexar leans down and presses a kiss to my head. I blink back tears at the tenderness.

"I want you," he says.

Dexar

I leave Alexis sleeping in my bed, where she belongs. It takes me a long moment before I can turn and walk away. My legs are feeling much better thanks to the salve Elliz and the other healers create for these types of injuries.

Tumbling Alexis...

There is nothing like it. Never has my body burned, almost insatiable with longing. Prior to this, females have been enjoyable distractions. But Alexis...

She is everything.

I walk to the large tashiv that serves as our prison. The air is cool this morning, and tribe members are keeping their voices to low murmurs, likely shocked at such an attack.

Brix strides toward me, and we both study the tashiv.

It is rare that this structure is used for anything other than the occasional discipline for warriors who have challenged each other after too much noptri.

Today, though, it holds the traitor who thought to kill my Lexi in front of me.

"What do we know?" I ask.

Brix glances behind me, and I gesture to my guards, who move away, out of earshot.

"Orcan is the traitor, qatai."

My heart stops, and I stare at Brix. For a moment, I wonder if he is joking, but his eyes hold no humor.

They hold nothing but cold retribution.

Orcan has been one of my advisers for years. This seems impossible.

"Are you sure?"

"He has confessed, qatai. He was seen close to the kradi just a few moments before it went up in flames."

Perhaps he confessed under torture. Just because he was in the area doesn't necessarily mean—

"He was carrying a tresla pod," Brix continues. "The only reason we thought to question him is because the Krinir boy recognized the pod and asked Zarix if we were preparing for an attack."

"Javir," I murmur, still attempting to accept this reality.

"Javir. Apparently, the tresla pods were used to fight off the Voildi during the attack on Tecar's camp. The boy grew concerned, wondering if we were about to be invaded. He asked Zarix, and when the kradi exploded, Zarix insisted we question Orcan."

"A mere coincidence," I murmur, and Brix nods.

"Without the boy noticing the pod, there would be nothing tying Orcan to the explosion and no reason to question him."

"Why did he do it?" This is what I can't understand.

"He was one of the warriors who left Lafa's tribe. While he swore allegiance to us, he has obviously been passing information to Lafa. For years."

I growl at the thought. It makes sense now—why Orcan refused to agree that Lafa could be working with the Voildi.

"And now Lafa is dead," I say.

"Yes. But he knew about what the arrival of the human females would mean. As soon as he learned that they were here, he must have focused on attaining them himself. Since Varic was his second-in-command, it's likely that Lafa shared this plan with him."

"And Orcan decided that neither I nor Varic should have Alexis."

Brix nods silently, casting me a slightly wary look. I'm

shaking with rage, battling the urge to storm into the tashiv and slit Orcan's throat.

It takes me long moments before I am able to speak.

"I cannot go in there," I say. "I will kill him, and we need him alive, for now. Question him until you are sure you have everything he knows."

Brix nods. "Yes, qatai. May I make a suggestion?"

"Yes."

"You mentioned that Alexis wishes to travel close to the dragon's territory to look for signs of her friend."

I narrow my eyes at him. "This is correct."

"Have you considered that removing the female from this camp may be a good idea?"

I hold back the harsh words that want to rip from my throat. I can protect Alexis in my camp. This is now her home. She should be safe here.

But there have now been two attempts on her life.

"If I could guarantee that we would not be attacked, I would consider it."

Brix opens his mouth, obviously confused, and I clarify, "If Alexis were to leave, I would go with her."

I've clearly stunned the warrior because his mouth gapes for a moment while he searches for a reply.

"We have seen attempts on her life in this tribe. If Lafa can get to Orcan, he may have other traitors in this camp. Imagine if one of the warriors I send with Alexis is actually working for Varic." My chest tightens, my hands clenching at the thought.

Soon I will have to tell her why she is really here. And I don't believe she will forgive me for keeping the truth from her.

CHAPTER ELEVEN

A lexis

"You want to what?"

Zarix raises an eyebrow, but his jaw juts out stubbornly. I grin at him. It looks like the big guy is coming precariously close to blushing.

"Beth talks about the place she danced with such longing," he says, his voice gruff. "I wish to recreate this for her here."

My heart. It's melting.

"That's adorable. She'll love it. So what do you need from me?"

"I do not know what this will look like or what she needs. I was hoping you would."

I grin. "It just so happens that I can help."

When I was eight, I was moved to a foster family that seemed promising. Julie—the mom—had always wanted a "little girl" for her to dress up. The problem? By that age, I'd lost the cheerful innocence that most young girls have. I hated dressing up, and the woman was continually embarrassed by my refusal to play by her rules. I had no idea what those rules were, but I knew I was failing. The one bright spot was the dance classes she insisted I take. I had no real skill, but I loved learning the different positions.

Six months later, Julie gave up. She and Brian, my foster dad, decided they didn't really want me after all. There were no more dance classes.

We're standing close to the mishua pen, which I'm not technically supposed to be near, but Zarix found me staring at the smoking ruin of my research kradi. He gave me a sympathetic look and then asked if I could help him with something.

Of course I was intrigued.

"Okay. First, you'll need a space that's large enough for a proper dance floor. Do you have that?"

"How large does it need to be?"

I point at the kradi where the mishua food is kept. "I'm guessing you'll want it to be at least that big. Beth is a ballet dancer, which means lots of leaping and twirling. You need space for that."

Zarix narrows his eyes at the kradi thoughtfully. "I believe I have something that could work."

"Oh yeah?"

"I am owed a large space in Dexar's kradi. Do you think Beth would like that?"

He's nervous. I smile at him. "Beth will be stoked at how thoughtful you are. But yes, it sounds great. She'll be away from prying eyes, but if she wants to, she can invite people in to see her dance."

"Perhaps she would like to teach others to dance one day."

I nod. "Yeah, I can imagine she'd love that. Okay, so you've got the space. You need the floor to be soft enough that she can land on it without damaging her joints, but it needs to be completely flat. The floor beneath Dexar's kradi seems pretty good, but you'll need to check this with Beth once you've surprised her. You'll need a barre too," I muse.

"A barre."

Zarix's brow furrows, and I tear a small piece of paper from the stack in my hands. I lean on the wall enclosing the mishua and attempt a rough sketch of a dance studio.

"See this long thing here? It'll need to run along one of the walls. It needs to be strong enough that she can use it to warm up and stretch."

Zarix nods. "And what is this?"

"That's a mirror. Dancers need to be able to see themselves as they move."

"Anything else?"

I shrug. "I don't think so, but I'm not a dancer. If you can get these things sorted, Beth will be ecstatic."

He grins, and I blink at him. Zarix is a serious guy, but when he's around Beth or Javir, his grumpy facade cracks. Obviously, the idea of Beth being pleased with him is enough for him to loosen up a bit.

"Thank you, Alexis," he says. "Is there any way I can repay you?"

I shake my head. "Just make Beth happy."

"I will," he nods solemnly, his eyes serious. "I promise. Let me know if you need anything."

I smile, and he wanders off to get to work, leaving me staring at the mishua. Three warriors are currently dealing with a mishua who does not seem happy about the giant cart they're attempting to hook up to her. The mishua snorts, and one of the warriors steps forward, talking to her sternly. The cart is being loaded with food and other goods for trade with another tribe.

I barely hold back a laugh as the mishua lowers her head threateningly. Zarix glances into the pen as he walks past and jumps over the wall. He strides toward the mishua and says a few words to her, and she instantly quits misbehaving.

Zarix is a good guy. I'm glad Beth is so happy here. And Nevada, and Ellie. But my heart hurts at the reminder that I'm once again on the outside looking in.

I learned young that the happily ever afters I saw on bad Lifetime movies are not for people like me. Expecting anything else is just a way to get your hopes crushed.

Dexar's face flashes in front of my eyes, and I turn away from the weapons kradi, making my way along the path toward our rooms. Dexar has shown no inclination to allow me to move back to my own rooms, and truthfully, I haven't protested all that much.

As much as he insists on "his way or the highway," Dexar treats me well. If anything, we *fit* together in a way I never imagined when he smiled at me from his throne just a few weeks ago.

But ultimately, we're from divergent worlds. I snort. Literally. But even if you disregard the whole Earth versus Agron thing, Dexar and I couldn't be more different.

I'm the underdog. The foster kid who had to study night and day so I could get a scholarship, which still didn't cover enough of my college expenses for me to quit my full-time job. Dexar was raised knowing he'd rule over thousands of people and taught from a young age that he was special.

What do a scrappy foster kid and an alien king have in common?

Nothing.

Dexar is sitting at the table when I arrive, ready for lunch.

"How are your legs?" I ask.

"Fine."

I stare him down, and he sighs.

"They feel much better, Alexis. Now, how about you tell me what you were doing near the weapons kradi today?"

I glower at him. "Spies, Your Majesty?"

"Just concerned tribe members."

I roll my eyes. "I was talking to Zarix. He's planning a surprise for Beth, and he needed my help."

A flash of jealousy crosses his face, and I raise an eyebrow. He seems to grapple with it and then finally nods, passing me back my plate, which is heavy on the greens I like and light on the root vegetable I don't. I attempt to ignore the warm feeling rising in my chest. This guy misses nothing.

I've been avoiding Dexar for the past few days. Sex with him was incredible, but lying next to him and opening up to him about my childhood? That was dangerous. And listening to him talk about *why* he's so committed to growing his tribe? That was stupid.

If I'm going to have sex with Dexar—which, let's face it, I sure as hell am—it needs to be just sex. No snuggling and talking after.

My heart can't risk it.

"So," I say, reaching for my cup. "We never finished our discussion about the favor you owe me."

Dexar narrows his eyes, and I grin.

"When *are* Beth and Zarix going to be mated anyway?"

"They wish to wait until the other human females have been found," he says.

My grin widens. "I hate to say 'I told you so.'" He snorts,

and I wink at him. "As per our agreement, you have to give me something that I want. And I want to go explore the area near the dragon's territory."

He raises one eyebrow, but I can see the refusal on his face. I grit my teeth.

"You know this isn't going to happen," he tells me, and I narrow my eyes at him.

"Our agreement is that I wouldn't leave the tribe for good," I say. "You said nothing about leaving and then returning."

"There have been two attempts on your life here at camp. You think I'm going to allow you to leave when you could be attacked at any moment?"

"So come with me," I say. "Unless you're scared."

He stares at me, eyes narrowing in offense. "Scared?"

I hold back my grin. "Yeah, scared to leave the comfort of this kradi."

He snorts, and I continue.

"You, Your Majesty, are spoiled. You probably couldn't survive a few nights in the wild without all the bowing and scraping of your court. What would you possibly do if you didn't have a servant to tuck you in every night?"

He frowns in confusion and grits his teeth as the device in his ear obviously translates for him. Then his lips curl in a slow grin as he gives me a heated look.

"I would have you 'tuck me in,' of course."

I huff out a breath. "You're not funny," I say even as my lips tremble.

"I would like nothing more than to disappear with you away from all this," he says suddenly, and his voice is serious, his eyes intent.

I squirm, glancing away. "But?"

"But I won't risk your life."

I open my mouth, and he holds up a hand.

"Do you trust me?"

I hesitate, and his face shuts down, eyes becoming blank.

"Hold on," I say. "Give me a moment."

He nods, his expression once again bored, but I didn't miss the flash of hurt in his eyes. He takes a bite, watching me as I think.

"I trust you to keep your word," I say finally. "But you're sneaky, Dexar. You're way more experienced at these kinds of bargains than I am."

His eyes lighten slightly, although his face is still hard. "I have no doubt you can keep up, Lexi." His voice is low, and from the way he runs his gaze over my body, he's remembering how well I kept up a few nights ago.

I blush, and he laughs, relaxing back in his chair as he picks up his cup and takes a sip.

"You will give me your map, and I will give it to one of my most trusted warriors." He holds up a hand as I open my mouth to protest, and I slam it shut, gritting my teeth. "He will take five men to this area, and they will study it for any signs of your missing friend or the dragon. If they concede that either of them have recently been in the area, I will personally travel with you once Varic is no longer a threat."

I raise my eyebrows. That's more than I expected. Beth told me all about Varic and how he's decided that he's now a qatai. The guy sounds like a garden-variety sociopath.

"Here's the problem I have with that. We don't know how long Varic will still be a threat. We don't have weeks or months to wait."

Dexar narrows his eyes at me. "If your friend is somehow still alive, there is no reason to believe that the dragon will suddenly kill her within a few weeks. Besides, Varic will not be a problem for much longer."

I think it over. "You don't think Charlie is still alive."

"No, I don't. But if you do, I will do this for you."

I blow out a breath. "Fine. I agree. You know, there's something I've been wondering about for a while. You never seemed surprised by the fact that we landed on your planet," I say. "Rakiz and Terex were stunned, and it took them a while to come to terms with it. But you never seemed surprised. Why is that?"

He looks surprised now and strangely discomforted. "I find that I do not want to tell you."

"Why?"

"Because it will give you another reason to want to leave this camp."

Now I'm really curious. "Please tell me." I say it simply, and Dexar sighs.

"Your ship is not the first to crash-land on this planet."

"What?" My pulse begins to race. "When did the other ship crash?"

"Approximately forty revolutions ago." Dexar is watching me carefully, which is the only reason I'm able to prevent myself from getting up to pace. I need to burn off this excitement somehow, and I start tapping my foot lightly on the ground.

"Where is it? I want to see it."

Dexar narrows his eyes at me. "Why?"

I stay silent. Because even if it's been crashed for forty years, it may have parts that I can salvage to use on our other ship. Depending on the type of ship and where it came from, of course.

Dexar tilts his head at me knowingly, obviously reading my mind. "And that is why."

"At least tell me where it is."

"Close to where you think the dragon's territory is located."

I stare at him. "And what happened to the people on that ship?"

He shrugs. "They were all dead when my father arrived."

My mind is racing as we finish our meal. I get to my feet, moving toward the bathroom so I can wash my hands. Dexar's hand whips out, grabbing my wrist and pulling me close.

"Hey!"

"Remember our agreement, Lexi. I have trusted you with this information. Do not think to sneak out of my camp."

I roll my eyes. "I told you, I agree with your plan to get rid of Varic before we go anywhere."

I widen my eyes innocently at him. After Varic is no longer a threat, all bets are off.

He studies my face, and finally his mouth tips up in a slow grin. "Ah, Lexi," he says, and my nipples harden at his low voice and the dirty promises in his eyes. "With you, I am never bored."

I raise one eyebrow, and he laughs, leaning close to nibble along my neck. I close my eyes with a sigh.

I'm never bored with him either.

Dexar gets to his feet with me still clutched securely in his arms. His eyes are dark, and I feel like I'm already naked as he moves back toward his bedroom, his gaze on my face the entire time.

He places me on his bed, and I shiver at the look in his eyes. He moves with a restrained power as he pulls off his shirt, and my gaze moves greedily over his chest.

God, the guy is built.

He reaches for his pants, and I don't waste time. I unlace

my dress, racing him as he crawls onto the bed, suddenly naked. He reaches for me, and within moments, my dress is gone.

He freezes, and I glance down. His eyes widen as he brushes my tattoo with his fingers, entranced.

I'm completely naked, but it's this that makes me blush. He runs his lips over the ink and raises his head, confusion in his eyes as it doesn't smudge.

"It's a tattoo."

He repeats the word, and suddenly the lethally handsome alien king is...cute.

I grin. "It's an atom. I'm kind of a geek."

He returns his attention to the tattoo. "How did I miss this?"

I blush again as I instantly get a visual of the way I crouched over his face last time we were busy in this bed.

"You were, uh...focused on other things."

My atom is designed to look like a compass, and it curves up my hip, reminding me once again of my commitment to get home.

Then Dexar kisses his way along my hip and across the sensitive skin of my stomach. He moves up my body, his arms sliding beneath me as his body cages mine. My breath quickens, and he drops his gaze down to my breasts, suddenly predatory.

Lust hits me like a drug, and I'm instantly heavy-lidded as he drops kisses along the tops of my breasts, then finally, finally, he leans up and kisses me, his lips hot as he steals my breath.

His tongue presses into my mouth, possessing, enticing, and encouraging me to kiss him back.

I groan, pouring everything I have into our kiss.

He chuckles against me, and I suddenly need to turn the

tables. I slide my hand down, finding the hard length of his cock, and his whole body tenses as I run my hand up and down his shaft.

He pulls away, staring down at me. Then he leans down, sucking at my nipples, alternating between them as he grazes them with his teeth. Pleasure bursts through me, and I shiver, groaning as my muscles turn to water and I throw my head back.

He slides his hand down, over my sensitive folds and into the place where I want him most. He drags his slick fingers back up, stroking my clit, and I grind against those clever fingers, already close to climax.

"Now," I choke out. "Now, now, now, now."

He laughs, but it's tight, his voice hoarse as he positions himself before finally thrusting inside me. He pulls back and thrusts again, and I arch my back, writhing against him as I pull his head close, running my teeth down his neck.

He curses, and I grin, and then I'm gripping his back, urging him on as he speeds up, thrusting faster and faster as he rocks into me.

My body clamps down, and I gasp as contractions of bliss hit me. I cry out as my orgasm goes on and on, and Dexar thrusts once more, his body shaking as he empties himself inside me.

I rest my eyes as Dexar rolls, pulling me close until I'm sprawled over his chest.

I sit on the top of the stairs, hidden in the shadows. I've been here for six months, but I'm doing it wrong. Whatever "it" is.

"You had one job. Give me a fucking kid. Not only did you fail at that, but you decided the best idea was to raise someone else's mutt?"

I flinch, betrayal ripping through me like a knife. I like Brian. He never makes me call him Dad. He took me fishing once and taught me how to reel in a small fish with seemingly infinite patience.

But he's just like all the others.

"She had one purpose. Make us a family. The kid barely even speaks!"

"You wanted her too, Brian." Julie's voice is shaky, but I know what's going to happen next.

I creep back upstairs and begin to pack.

I jolt awake, frowning. I didn't think I was tired enough to fall asleep, and I shake off the memories that cling to me like spiderwebs. Talking to Dexar about my childhood has opened up Pandora's box. Now I need to close it down.

I roll off his chest, ignoring his hand as he reaches for me.

"I'm sure you've got things to do," I mutter, pulling my dress back on.

Dexar watches me out of dark eyes. "Are you okay?"

"I'm fine. I'll see you later."

Dexar

Alexis is pulling away. Even a blind male could see that she is determined to not feel anything for me. Her vacant smile when we finished tumbling and the way she has been spending less time in my rooms make it clear that she has no intention of being my qatal.

I am attempting to be patient.

Lexi was abandoned when she was just hours old. This means that she is likely wary of being hurt again. My hands fist at the thought of whoever could leave behind such a precious gift.

So how do I convince her that I will not hurt her?

Perhaps you should start with being honest.

I rub at the back of my neck, glowering at the exit that Alexis just strode through. If I tell her about the prophecy, she will leave me. Perhaps not today, perhaps not even tomorrow, but she will never trust that my feelings for her are real.

I sigh. While I have attempted to keep Alexis close, I don't want her to feel smothered by me. She is used to being independent, my Lexi. Now she is watched wherever she goes, by warriors who are ready to jump into action and protect her from any possible harm at a moment's notice.

She's allowing it. For now.

I spend the afternoon hearing petitions in the Great Room. But I am noticeably distracted, and I'm instantly alert when a warrior steps into the room, moving to Brix and whispering in his ear.

Brix's gaze flicks to mine, and I lunge to my feet, striding toward him as the room goes silent.

"What happened?"

He glances around us and gestures toward the entrance. I run my gaze over those who are still waiting to bring me their issues and problems.

"I have an emergency. This will continue tomorrow."

Murmurs break out, but I ignore them, stalking out of the kradi with Brix.

"What happened? Is it Alexis?

"She is fine. But...she is with your mother."

I close my eyes as I curse. My mother isn't the problem. It's the female who spends such large amounts of time with my mother that worries me.

I jump into action, striding through the camp. My mother's kradi is large, with a small garden outside, overlooking the river. She refuses to move into my kradi, insisting that she spent many revolutions surrounded by the tribe and now prefers privacy.

As much as the security risk unsettles me, I understand her need for her own space.

The three women are sitting in the garden when I arrive, deep in conversation. My mother is sitting close to Alexis, who is now pale as she stares at Ini in horror.

Ini is the wisewoman, and I never intended for the two to meet. At least not until I had explained to Alexis why she is here.

I close my eyes briefly, wrestling with fury, and then stalk forward. Alexis visibly stiffens, her gaze immediately finds my face, and her shock and dismay transforms to anger.

"You!" she spits, and my mother jolts for a moment, staring at Alexis in shock. The shock turns to amusement as Alexis gets to her feet, hands fisted as she stares me down.

"I suggest we take this to a more secluded location," I begin, and Alexis lets out a choked laugh.

"Why bother when everyone in this tribe knows exactly why I'm here?" Her voice hardens further. "You know, I wondered why people kept calling me qatal. I figured it was a polite term for the qatai's girlfriend or something."

"Alexis—"

"But no. They're calling me that because of some stupid prophecy."

Ini clears her throat, but her eyes are dancing with amusement, not narrowed in offense.

My mother gives me a look of rebuke. I can practically hear her asking me why I failed to inform Alexis of the prophecy.

"One year," Alexis hisses. "You said I could go home in one revolution!"

I wave my hand as I step forward, lowering my voice. "Yes," I say silkily, fury beating a drum inside my head. "One revolution. So look me in the eyes and tell me you would not leave me at the first opportunity."

"Dexar—"

"Deny it. Deny it, my little liar."

Alexis's mouth drops open, and my mother shakes her head at me, closing her eyes for a brief moment. Ini looks even more amused, her wrinkled mouth trembling as she holds back a grin.

"You're calling *me* a liar right now?" Alexis gapes at me.

I give her a look. "What would you have had me do?"

"Uh, maybe when I asked you what the hell Nara was talking about when she insisted she was the *chosen one*, you could've told me? Or any time I expressed confusion about why the hell a random human woman was being targeted by your enemies, you could've said, 'Oh hey, Alexis, they think that fate sent you here,'" she snaps.

"And then what?"

"And then maybe I would've thought twice before sleeping with you, you arrogant jackass!"

My mother shoots me an amused look, and Alexis follows my gaze, her cheeks turning red.

"You have a purpose here, child," Ini says, and Alexis flinches, her face draining of color. I frown at her, unable to understand the haunted look in her eyes.

I reach forward and grab her hand, shooting Ini a dark look as I pull Alexis into the kradi.

"You did think twice," I murmur. "You pushed me away at every opportunity, even when it became evident that we were right for each other."

She lets out a bitter laugh. "Right for each other? Why? Because I'm 'light of eyes and white of hair'? You don't actually want me, Dexar. You never wanted me. From the moment you saw me, you saw a way to protect your tribe. Someone with a *purpose*."

Something about this word has wounded Alexis deeply, and I attempt to be patient.

"That's not true. From the moment I saw you, I wanted you for my own."

She rolls her eyes, and I reach for her, but she backs away, almost tripping over a chair.

"Don't touch me."

"Enough!" I growl. "Tell me, what would have happened if I had told you about the prophecy when we first met?"

"I would never have agreed to stay here."

"And sacrifice a chance to find your friend? I don't think so. You would have stayed, but you would have attempted to escape at every opportunity. And you never would have believed that I truly wanted you and not just because of the prophecy."

"Because you don't! I don't believe in prophecies, but you and all your people obviously do. God, I feel like an idiot, wandering around thinking people were just being nice to me when they really expect me to stay here with you so you can have one hundred revolutions of peace and prosperity!"

She throws up her hands, turning away, and I attempt to push down the panic that's rising. Alexis is looking at me as if I'm a stranger. As if she doesn't even know me.

"You are pushing me away because you are scared," I say. "Because you were abandoned and hurt again and again as a child. Is that the life you wish to return to?"

"You know nothing about me," she says quietly.

"I know you have a chance for happiness here, with me. I would be yours for the rest of your days, Alexis."

She immediately shakes her head, her shoulders hunching as if protecting her from my words. "You only want me because Ini gave you that prophecy when you were a kid," she says. "If you'd never heard it, you would've let me go when I arrived here. Admit it."

I'm silent for a long moment, and she nods.

I sigh. "Look at me. *Look at me*," I say, and she finally turns. "Was I immediately entranced when I saw you? Did I think of the prophecy? Yes. I won't deny it. But it only took a few moments with you for me to want *you*. I don't know what I have to do to make you believe this."

She's already shaking her head again, and I wrestle with my frustration.

Anger makes my words hard. "We are going around in circles. With time, you will see that you are the one for me." She snorts, and I grind my teeth, fury rising at her instant denial. "If you attempt to leave this planet, I will have both ships destroyed," I snarl, and she whirls, her hands fisting.

"You ruthless bastard. You'd do that to the other women?"

"*You* would do that to them. You may not believe me, but we are meant to be. Even without the prophecy. I will wait as long as it takes for you to accept this."

She laughs coldly. "You'll be waiting until hell freezes over," she says. Her eyes fill with tears, and I step forward, my chest tightening at her obvious hurt.

And then she turns and stalks out of the kradi.

CHAPTER TWELVE

A lexis

Betrayal makes my hands shake as I wander through the camp. I have nowhere to go—nowhere except back to Dexar's rooms.

I ignore the eyes on me as I walk with no destination in mind. I *knew* not to trust Dexar. After our conversation in bed, it was clear that every decision he makes is with the best interests of his tribe in mind.

"Alexis? Are you okay?" Beth takes my arm, her face sympathetic, and I realize my cheeks are wet. I reach up and brush off the tears, but more drip from my eyes. I'm a mess.

"No." I sniff.

"Come with me."

I keep my head down in an attempt to hide my devastation from curious eyes as we walk back toward Beth's kradi. The sun is warm on my skin, the breeze refreshing, and I suddenly want nothing more than a brutal storm to rage and reflect my meltdown.

Neither Javir nor Zarix are in the kradi, and Beth directs me to a huge pillow, handing me a small piece of cloth to wipe my face with.

I scrunch it into my hand and sob.

Beth's eyes fill with tears, and despite myself, I let out a watery laugh.

"I'm sorry," she mutters. "I'm terrible when other people are hurting. Do you want to tell me about it?"

I take a deep breath and blurt out the entire horrible story. My eyes sting when I'm finished, but I'm no longer crying. I've now moved on to cold fury.

Beth wraps her arm around me. "I've seen him look at you, Alexis. Do you truly believe he only wants you around for some weird prophecy?"

I shrug. "I don't know what to think. And I don't know why I suddenly care. I'm meant to be doing my time here until we can find Ivy and Charlie and get the hell off this planet. So why am I suddenly so devastated?"

Beth looks at me like I'm being particularly obtuse, and I frown at her.

"You obviously have deep feelings for Dexar," she says, "or you wouldn't be so hurt."

I'm instantly shaking my head, and she raises her eyebrows.

"Would you prefer if I left you to your denial?"

I narrow my eyes at her. "I feel like he manipulated me," I say, choosing to ignore that.

"Would anything have changed if you'd known about the prophecy?"

I stare down at the deep-green pillow beneath my butt. It reminds me of Dexar's eyes, and I scowl.

"I wouldn't have slept with him, that's for sure."

Beth snorts. "Really? You would've slept next to that fine man every night and you wouldn't have slept with him?"

"Shut up," I mutter, cheeks burning.

"You want to know what I think?"

"I dunno. You're kind of mean," I say, and she laughs.

"You were lying to him too, right? You had no intention of staying here for a year." She holds up her hands as I squint at her. "Just saying it like it is."

"Dexar said that too," I say. "But it's not the same."

"Really? Why?"

"'Cause he made me *feel* things! Things I thought he felt too! But they aren't even real."

She tilts her head. "How do you know they're not real? Did he say that?"

I sigh. "No, he said the opposite. But I let my guard down, Beth. And he hurt me."

"So now you get to decide how much it matters to you. If you could be guaranteed a long, happy life here with Dexar, would you take it?"

"I don't know."

"Tell me this, then. Why do you think he didn't tell you about the prophecy?"

"He said it was because I'd think he only wanted me here for that reason."

"And is that true?"

"Yes."

"So can you blame him for lying? If the guy truly has feelings for you—and anyone can see that he does—then he lied to you because he didn't want to hurt you. And because he knew you wouldn't believe him. Was he right?"

I pick at a loose thread hanging from the cushion. Truthfully, I've been pushing Dexar away since the moment we slept together and I realized that I was fascinated despite myself. I would've jumped at a reason to replace my growing attraction with anger.

"It doesn't make it right," I say stubbornly, but some of the heat has gone from my words, and now I just feel depressed and exhausted. "I hear what you're saying," I sigh. "I was lying to him too. So we're both a couple of lying liars who got caught out."

"You can see it that way. Or you can see it as you both trying to protect yourselves. And people only do that when they're scared to be vulnerable."

"How did you get so wise?"

Beth laughs, stretching her legs out on the floor in front of us. "Sometime between getting caught in that trap and agreeing to move back to this camp with Zarix, I realized how short life is. We survived something incredible, Alexis. The fact that we all made it through that crash is nothing short of a miracle, and finding the Braxians? That's just plain luck."

"Or fate," I murmur darkly, thinking of the stupid prophecy.

Beth laughs again, the sound musical. "Or fate. Whatever it is, we get a choice: Do we live in the now? Or do we hope for a future that we're not guaranteed?"

"Is that why you decided to stay?"

She shakes her head. "I decided to stay because the thought of being without Zarix was intolerable. If I were you, I'd imagine a life where you don't see Dexar ever again. If you're fine with that life, then you've got no problem. Shake off this prophecy shit and bide your time until you can get the hell outta dodge."

I attempt to ignore the denial that instantly shoots through me. "Do you think I overreacted?"

Beth shoots me a sympathetic look. "I think you reacted based on your life experience. Do you think Dexar will blame you for being upset? He was expecting it, which is why he didn't tell you. Was that a dumb move? Sure. But the guy's used to being in control one hundred percent of the time. He's probably floundering just as much as you are."

I sigh. Now that I've had some distance, I get it. I blew up at Dexar, proving that he was right not to tell me. Do I wish he'd told me sooner? Sure. But can I blame him? Not entirely.

"Being an adult really sucks sometimes," I mutter.

"It sure does. What are you going to do?"

"I'll give him a few hours to cool off, and then I'll go talk to him." I sigh. "Distract me. Tell me what's up with you?"

Beth grins. "Well, I have my lovely new dance studio. I believe I have you to thank for—hey!"

We both whirl as someone appears in the tent, and my mouth drops open.

"Tavis? What's wrong?"

He ignores me, and the hair on the back of my neck stands up as I stare at the sword in his hand. His eyes are cold as he looks at Beth, who is already scooting back on her butt as she reaches for a knife.

"Don't move," he says, striding forward and placing his sword close to my throat. I'm still frozen, sitting on the ground as I attempt to wrap my head around this new development.

Turns out Tavis isn't the blushing, bumbling kid he pretended to be.

Beth freezes, glancing at me wide-eyed.

"Are you going to kill me?" I ask, strangely calm.

"No. But if your friend doesn't stop looking for a weapon, she'll die next."

I choke at that. "Who did you kill?"

Please, God, tell me it's not Dexar. But no, I've seen Dexar train. There's no way Tavis could take him.

Unless he attacked him when he least expected it. Someone would've found his body by now though. Dexar is almost always surrounded by people.

Tavis ignores me, throwing a piece of material at Beth. "Put this in your mouth and tie it around your head."

Beth's hands are shaking as she ties the gag, and I glance around, frantically attempting to come up with anything that can get us out of this situation. Tavis is alert though, and the blade of his sword is so close to my neck that I barely dare to breathe.

Tavis drops a piece of rope in my lap. "Tie her hands."

I slowly move forward. Beth's smart, and she keeps her wrists apart while I tie her as loosely as I dare, attempting to make it look good. Hopefully, she'll be able to get out of here and get help as soon as we're gone.

It's all for nothing, though, because as soon as I finish, Tavis steps forward and backhands Beth across her head, and she slumps to the ground, unconscious.

"What are you doing? You could've killed her!"

Tavis smiles at me, and it's clear that he gives no fucks. "You're going to walk with me to the mishua pen as if we're just out for a stroll and Dexar put another guard on you. You're not going to say anything to anyone, or I'm going to make sure that Rowax comes in here and slits that female's throat. Understood?"

Rowax is in on this too?

"Understood," I grind out. I can see the writing on the wall. If Tavis isn't going to kill me, it's likely because he has something even worse in mind. Whatever it is, I'm unlikely to like it.

"Get up."

I slowly get to my knees, and Tavis stows his sword. I tense, and he shakes his head warningly, glancing at Beth. "Don't make me kill her."

"You're scum. Dexar's going to make you pay for this."

"Dexar will think you ran away."

I stare at him, and he smiles again. How did he fool me so easily? Reading people is my superpower. He's right though—after our argument this afternoon, Dexar will for sure assume I ran away.

Whatever. He needs me for his stupid prophecy. He'll hunt me down for sure.

Yup, I'm still not over it.

I grind my teeth as I walk toward the mishua pen. I don't know how Tavis is planning to get me out of here. The moment I'm seen getting on a mishua, someone will immediately inform Dexar.

"Wait here," Tavis says.

I wait, watching as Tavis walks into the mishua pen. All of a sudden, he's the shy, awkward, young warrior who asks another warrior for help as he pulls one of the mishua from the herd.

I shift on my feet, desperate to run. The problem? I don't know if Tavis is bluffing. If someone's watching me right now and they see me run, Beth could end up dead.

If she's not already.

No, Alexis, she's knocked out, that's all. Zarix will find her.

I tense as I watch Tavis saddling the mishua. Then he leaves her tied up and waiting, taking a few moments to joke with the other warrior before he moves back toward me.

"See that cart?" He points at it, and dread makes my hands shake. "You're going to wait for my signal, and then you're going to climb into it and cover yourself with the blanket."

"You son of a bitch."

He smiles at me, and I resist the urge to knee him in the nuts and run like hell. He's obviously going to pretend like he's been sent to trade with one of the other tribes.

By the time Dexar learns what has happened, we'll be long gone.

"Don't do anything stupid," he murmurs, lifting his hand as Brix walks past. Brix shakes his head at me, and I hope he's about to tell Dexar I was hanging out near the mishua.

We wait several more minutes, and I'm practically vibrating with the need to scream for help. Unfortunately, everyone's busy living their lives, barely paying me any attention. No one would ever suspect Tavis of something like this.

"Go," he tells me, and all of a sudden, he's not smiling anymore. This is it. He's feeling just as tense as I am, if not more, because if anyone catches him trying to take me out of here, he's dead.

I hesitate, and he keeps his eyes on the mishua as if we're discussing the beast. "Go now, or I'll make sure your friend suffers before she dies."

I go.

***

Dexar

Alexis is nowhere to be found.

I wasn't at all surprised when she didn't return for dinner, but she knows better than to avoid my kradi when it is time to sleep.

I spent a few minutes with my mother, reassuring her that I'll convince Alexis to see my side. My mother doesn't care about the prophecy. Oh, she wants the tribe to be safe, but she's mostly concerned with my happiness.

"I see how you two look at each other," she said as I watched Alexis stalk away. "Only true love can inspire such pain."

I scowled. I'm still attempting to come to terms with my feelings for Alexis, and she doesn't have any warm feelings left for me.

When I told my mother this, she laughed. "If Alexis didn't care for you, she wouldn't have been so upset. You've never had to work for female company, my darling. It pleases me to see that you have found your perfect match."

"Qatai?"

I turn, shaking off my mother's words.

"Yes?"

"The last time I saw her, she was near the mishua with Tavis," Brix says, and I grind my teeth. Alexis has obviously decided that none of our previous agreements matter anymore. Her actions confuse me though. The fierce female is not the type to back down from a fight. We both needed time to come to terms with the harsh words we exchanged, but I expected her to meet me in my rooms so we could continue our discussion.

Choosing not to return to my kradi is beneath her.

"I want the camp searched," I grind out. Brix nods, and we both turn at a high voice.

"Qatai," Yari says, out of breath as she reaches us. "You're needed in the healers' kradi."

Alexis.

I sprint toward the kradi, but it's not Alexis I find being

healed. It's Beth. Zarix's face is hard as stone, and he clutches Beth to him as if worried she will disappear.

"What happened?" I growl.

His voice is tight with fury as the healer bandages a deep cut on Beth's temple. "Tavis happened. He took Alexis and tied up Beth, hitting her hard enough in the head that he nearly cracked her skull."

Beth winces and lifts her hand, stroking it along his cheek. "Shh, baby, I'm okay, I promise."

Zarix doesn't seem convinced, but he falls silent as he presses a kiss to the top of her head.

I frown. "Tavis?"

Yari clears her throat, and I turn to her. "The young warrior who guarded the qatal's rooms, qatai."

"The one who cannot yet grow a beard?" I ask, shocked anew at the sheer ludicrousness.

"Yes, qatai."

He had us all fooled. And he took Alexis. I thought she was sulking, refusing to return to my kradi, when really she was being taken against her will. She must be terrified.

"When did they leave?"

"I noticed them before the evening meal," Brix says, his face hard.

"I do not blame you. This young warrior deceived us all," I reassure him, and he nods, but the guilt doesn't leave his eyes.

"Get me that adviser," I say. "The one who went up against Orcan."

"Andon."

"Yes. Tell him to bring everything he has about the possible locations of Varic's tribe. We ride tonight."

CHAPTER THIRTEEN

A lexis

It's hot and stuffy beneath the blanket, but Tavis has made it clear that if I push it off me, I'll regret it.

Not long after we left camp, I took my chance and rolled out of the cart before sprinting away from him. Tavis caught me, smacked me across the face, and tied my hands and feet.

I'm going to make him pay for this.

We've been traveling for at least a couple of hours because I've mentally relived every moment of my fight with Dexar multiple times. I've also alternated between composing my apology to him and repeatedly demanding an apology *from* him.

Beth's words run through my head. If I didn't care about Dexar an unreasonable amount, I wouldn't have felt so betrayed when I found out about the prophecy. I want him to want me for *me*. And yet, when he insisted that he does, I didn't believe him.

Dexar has no reason to lie to me. Realistically, if he wanted to keep me in his tribe, he could stick two massive guards on me and make sure I'm watched every moment of every day. Nothing in the prophecy specifies that I have to be happy. His words run through my mind on a loop, the frustration clear on his face.

"You may not believe me, but we are meant to be. Even without the prophecy. I will wait as long as it takes for you to accept this."

The problem? Both of us are damaged. He's had this prophecy hanging over his head since he was a kid, and it was drilled into him that he's responsible for the safety and security of his tribe.

And I learned early on that people can't be trusted.

When Ini talked about my *purpose*, I had an instant flashback to Brian's voice as he told Julie I hadn't fulfilled my purpose.

They hadn't invited me into their family because they wanted *me*. They'd wanted me to fill a space. Any kid could have done it, and when I hadn't measured up, they'd sent me back, a little more wounded and a whole lot less trusting.

Dexar was taught that what he wants doesn't really matter. I could've been ninety years old, and he'd still have been expected to mate with me. Regardless of how he felt about it.

And then, to his surprise, he wanted me. I think about the stunned pleasure in his eyes the night that I rode him, and my cheeks heat beneath the scratchy blanket. We gradually spent more and more time together, realizing that as much as we butt heads, we also spar, laugh, and bargain.

What must it have been like for him—to be feeling for me but to know that if I found out about the prophecy, I'd no longer trust him?

He was right. I *was* pushing him away. Because deep down, I never trusted that someone like him could truly want someone like me—the reject whose own parents hadn't loved her enough to keep her. The kid who was passed around—as unwanted as a worn-out thrift-store cardigan.

"*I want you,*" Dexar said in his low voice. And for a moment, I believed him. Then I shook it off, changing the subject to something lighter.

I blow out a breath, depressed. Now I'm being kidnapped by a guy who had me fooled into thinking he was about as confident as a substitute teacher on his first day at work.

Awesome.

If I get out of this alive, I'm telling Dexar how I feel.

Eventually, I must doze off because I wake to voices above my head.

"I have a delivery for Varic," Tavis says, and he sounds so pleased with himself that I want to wrap my hands around his throat.

Another warrior replies, but his voice is too low for me to hear. Then we're moving again, and voices surround the cart as we finally come to a stop.

Someone rips the blanket off me, and I have a moment to blink up at the star-studded sky before I'm dragged out of the cart.

I fall on my ass, and chortles sound around me. They instantly fall silent as another warrior approaches. He's shorter than Dexar and Zarix, but he's still built like a brick shithouse, with bulging muscles and no real neck to speak of. His eyes are hard as they examine me, and I shiver as he nods approvingly.

"I'm guessing you must be Varic," I mutter. I gesture to my feet, which are still tied. "Do you mind?"

He glances at one of the other warriors, and the guy cuts the rope on my feet while I suppress the urge to kick him in the face. Then he grabs me by the rope on my wrist and hauls me to my feet.

"Ow," I mutter as the rope digs into my skin. But I keep my eyes on Varic, who looks coolly amused as the Braxian cuts the rope off my wrists.

"What do you want?" I ask him, and he tilts his head.

"I assume you've heard of the prophecy?"

I scowl at him. "Yeah, I was recently introduced to it."

"Some say that you are destined to be the qatal of Dexar's tribe. However, if you examine the wording of the prophecy, it doesn't say this at all. Dexar's tribe is not the only tribe to use the word *qatai*. This is just another term for *tribe king*. That means that any tribe king can mate with you and be rewarded with one hundred years of peace and prosperity."

Oh boy. "And you think I'm just going to go along with this?"

His eyes are blank as he shrugs. "Your agreement is not required."

Varic turns to Tavis. "Does anyone know you took her?"

"No, qatai. I was trusted."

I grind my teeth. Damn fucking right he was.

"Did you do as I asked?"

"Yes, qatai. Rowax is dead."

I freeze. Tavis told me Rowax was on his side and ready to kill Beth at a moment's notice. Why would he kill him?

Varic nods. Then his hand is a blur as he swipes out with a long knife, slashing Tavis's throat.

I scream, backing away as his blood gushes out, and Tavis slumps to the ground, choking. It's over in moments, and I feel the blood drain from my face as I stare at Varic, who raises his eyebrow at me.

"Why?" My voice is a croak, and I wipe at my face, swallowing bile when my hand comes away red with Tavis's blood.

"He spent too long in Dexar's tribe. I can no longer trust his loyalties."

"He kidnapped me. He couldn't ever have shown his face there again."

Varic laughs. "He has betrayed you and you still would not kill him?"

"No."

"Well, as my mate, you will be treated well. I will be happy to indulge you in certain things if you behave. You feel the need to spare the lives of traitors? It will be done."

He has a twinkle in his eye that tells me those traitors would rather be dead.

I ignore his mate talk. No point indulging his insanity. "And Rowax?"

"Rowax also grew up in Lafa's tribe. He was encouraged to provide us with information about Dexar and chose not to."

I stare at him, stunned. This guy is a pure psychopath. I glance around at the other warriors encircling me, and not one of them seems surprised by this turn of events.

"Dexar is going to make you pay for this," I say.

Varic laughs and gestures to one of the warriors, who grabs my arm, pulling me away.

I don't struggle, allowing him to haul me through their

camp. It's much smaller than Dexar's camp, and I crane my neck, scanning my surroundings. Like every other Braxian camp I've seen, this camp is located next to the river. While it's dark, I can hear the water rushing over the rocks.

Worst-case scenario, I can take a page out of Beth's book, jump into the river, and hope for the best.

I shiver at the thought. None of my foster parents were real concerned about teaching me how to swim. I picked up the basics as a teenager, but I'm definitely not a strong swimmer.

"So," I murmur to the warrior as he pulls me to a kradi close to the river. "You want to help me get out of here? Dexar will make it worth your while."

He snorts, pushing me into the kradi.

"Tall, dark, and silent, huh? All I'm saying is that this is not gonna end well for you guys. If you want to guarantee you'll live, I suggest you let me go."

"Do you want me to gag you?"

I'm immediately shaking my head, and I pretend to zip my lips, although he obviously doesn't get the reference. The kradi is completely empty of all furniture, but a long metal pole is buried deep within the ground.

"Sit," he says warningly.

I sit.

He pulls out more rope, and I sigh. This time, I push my elbows back against my ribs as I hold out my hands—the picture of submissiveness. He walks out of the kradi, leaving me tied to the long metal pole, and I stare at it while I wiggle my wrists.

Yup. More than enough slack to get free. But I'm not going to risk sneaking out of here in the dark while those warriors celebrate with their sociopathic leader. With my luck, I'd probably trip and break an ankle or end up falling into the river.

My best bet is to wait until these guys go to sleep and the sun begins to rise. Then I'm hauling ass out of here.

I have no idea how to get back to Dexar's camp, but all I have to do is get away from these assholes. He'll find me.

I know he will.

Dexar

"There are two possible locations for Varic's tribe," Andon says, pointing to the large map spread over the table. "Here and here."

"What makes you so certain?"

"These are the most sheltered locations, close to running water and removed enough from territory held by either Rakiz or yourself, qatai."

I wrestle with my impatience. Alexis has been gone for hours now. I must choose correctly.

"If I were Varic, I would choose this one." Brix points to the location furthest from our tribe. "It's out of the way but close enough to the Seinex Forest for him to pick up stragglers who fled Lafa's attack."

Andon nods. "I agree. However, we can't underestimate him. He may be aware that we would determine that this is his most likely location. And in that case, he will choose the location that is closer to your tribe but further west—unlikely to be discovered by Rakiz's hunters."

I contemplate the map for long moments, finally giving in and pacing as I think it over. Alexis's face continues to appear in front of my eyes, her expression haunted as she pleads with me to find her.

I snort. Alexis is more likely to demand that I "hurry up and slap some motherfuckers around." I know my Lexi, and she'll be taking this in stride. My biggest fear is her smart mouth. I would bet my favorite knife that she is mocking Varic, likely pushing him and pushing him as she searches for any weaknesses that she can use.

Varic is ruthless. He could hurt her. Perhaps even damage her permanently.

My stomach clenches at the thought, and I force myself to concentrate.

"Split our warriors into two groups." I point to the second location. "I will go here with Brix and five hundred of our most experienced fighters. Send another five hundred to the location furthest away, just in case."

Andon nods. "Yes, qatai." He moves away to relay my orders, and I turn to Brix.

"How is Rowax?"

"He is still alive, qatai. He lost a lot of blood."

"Tell me when he is conscious. I want to speak to him."

***

Alexis

I doze. When I open my eyes, Varic is standing in the kradi, staring at me like a creeper.

"What?" I growl, and he tilts his head again, as if he doesn't quite know what to do with me. I snort. He thinks mating with me will guarantee that this little tribe of outlaws will have prosperity?

When I'm through with him, he'll be begging Dexar to take me back.

"You don't seem to be afraid of me," he says finally. "Why is this? Are you brave or merely stupid?"

I lick my dry lips, desperate for water at this point. "You can't kill me if you want me to fulfill your stupid prophecy."

"I may not be able to kill you, but you don't have to be in perfect health when I take you as my mate."

I smile at him. "You know what's interesting about humans?" He stays silent, and I bare my teeth at him as I widen my smile. "We're much, much more fragile than Braxians. In fact, it's a wonder I'm alive at all after so long without water. If you're not careful, I may end up dying just to spite you."

He growls, but I see his eyes widen as he whirls, stepping out of the kradi. A few moments later, he hands me a cup of water. I gulp it down before handing it back to him.

"So," I say. "Since you're planning to be my sugar woogums, how about you tell me why you're doing this?"

Varic raises his eyebrow but finally shrugs. "Some people are born with everything they could ever want, while others are born to take it."

"I'm guessing you're firmly in the second category."

He ignores me. "Take Dexar, for example. Our fathers were friends. Did you know?"

I shake my head, clamping down on the urge to inform him that absolutely no one talks about him or his father.

"Dexar's father was the qatai. The most respected tribe king. My father was nothing but his underling."

"I thought they were friends?"

"Silence." His voice is suddenly harsh, a weird light entering his eyes, and I shut my mouth.

"Eventually," he says, "my father realized he would never

know true power while he was a member of Dexar's tribe. He left to join Lafa's tribe, working his way up the ranks until he was once again second only to the qatai."

I sigh. It doesn't take a psychologist to see where this is going.

Varic is almost unrecognizable right now, his face a dark red, his hands clenched into fists. He looks nothing like the composed, logical man who murdered Tavis in cold blood just a few hours ago. He steps forward, and my hands itch to grab the jeweled knife attached to his belt.

"I'm guessing you weren't a fan of that," I offer, and he ignores me.

"Both my father and Lafa died while battling Tecar's tribe. I saw my chance and took it. Most Braxians would never willingly partner with the Voildi. As soon as Lafa was dead, I learned how he had died." He smiles, and I shiver.

"He tried to kill my friends."

Varic nods. "Your human friends. 'The ones from the stars,'" he quotes, and I grind my teeth.

"I knew of the prophecy. Anyone who had spoken to Dexar's father for more than a few moments had heard of it," Varic sneers. "He was so proud, assuming his son would mate with the one who would guarantee peace and prosperity."

He nods toward my light-blonde hair, and for the tenth time in the past few days, I wish I'd dyed it dark when I was on Earth.

"It only took a few days to learn of you and of your deal with Dexar," he says.

"So now what? You think you'll mate with me and somehow secure prosperity for your sad band of misfits?"

The deranged light leaves his eyes, and he looks less like a raving lunatic and more like the sociopath I met last night.

The sociopath is scarier.

"It doesn't matter if the prophecy is true," he says. "It matters that Braxians believe it is true. I have already gathered more people than I could have imagined, all of them ready for a new world order. Why should those of us equipped to rule be left out in the cold simply because others were born to royalty?"

I narrow my eyes at him. "Dexar's father built his tribe from nothing. What makes you think you'd be able to do any better? What makes you qualified to rule?"

"I know what is best for our people. And it is not joining with the Voildi or bowing to Dexar's tribe simply because it is larger and wealthier. I will kill Dexar, and his tribe will become mine."

I ignore the panic that clutches at my chest and roll my eyes. "So you'll share your power equally amongst each of your tribe members, then?"

He instantly shakes his head, and I laugh.

"This would not work," he begins, and I snort.

"You can't put a cherry on a pile of shit and call it a sundae." He frowns, and I clarify, "This isn't about creating democracy or taking down a ruthless dictator. This is about you clawing your way to power, however you can."

"Think what you will. Your future will remain the same regardless." His voice is remote, as if he's reading from a script, and he turns away, obviously bored of our conversation.

"I'll have food sent to you," he says as he walks out.

CHAPTER FOURTEEN

A lexis

I'm given a small meal of bread and some waxy cheese, and then the warrior who tied me up appears. My window of opportunity has disappeared. Do these people not sleep at all?

The sun is rising, brushing the ground with rosy-fingered rays as I step into the fresh air. This part of the river is wider than I imagined, the water rushing by so fast that it's a blur.

I'm glad I didn't jump in.

In the distance, mountains loom, impressively craggy with no snow to be seen. I wonder if we're close to the dragon's territory.

"Walk," the warrior orders, and I roll my eyes but move faster. He takes me just a few kradis down from the one I was kept in, and I widen my eyes at the women who are all squeezed into the small space. There are just a few chairs in here along with a tiny bathtub, and most of the women are sitting on the floor, staring at me.

"I will be outside," the warrior tells me, the warning clear. No funny business. He cuts the rope around my wrists, and I wince as I rub my hands over the marks on my skin. Then I'm left alone with what must be ten or twelve women.

One of them steps forward.

"We have drawn a bath for you, qatal," she says, and I flinch at the word. I'm suddenly so homesick for Dexar's tribe that I could cry. I want nothing more than to be sparring with him over lunch, watching him hear petitions in the Great Room, or curled up next to him in his huge bed.

"Don't call me that."

"As you wish, qatal."

I roll my eyes again. "Are you guys going to help me get out of here or what? You know Dexar's probably on his way here by now, right? And boy is he going to be pissed."

I catch one of the women in the corner going pale, but the woman in front of me narrows her eyes. Her face is worn, but her eyes are dark and hard, reminding me of an eagle. She looks like someone who has seen some shit and doesn't want to see any more.

"No one will help you," Eagle Eyes tells me softly, although her tone is firm. "The people here have seen too much suffering to refuse what the fates have so generously provided."

I stare at her. "You're about to see more suffering. You know that, right?" I'm suddenly desperate for her to see sense. "I've seen Dexar's warriors training, and they're going to rip through this camp like a tornado until they find me. This won't end happily for Varic."

Another woman speaks up. This one is heavily pregnant and sitting in one of the few chairs. "We have fought battle after battle, always losing. Our warriors are few, and our qatai promised us that if we put our faith in him, we would be able to live peaceful lives."

"You want peaceful lives? Join Dexar's tribe."

"Dexar is a monster," another woman hisses, and I turn, stunned at the venom in her tone. She's got long, gorgeous black hair, although it's tangled and greasy. "His tribe is already large and prosperous, but it's not enough for him. He still took you and thinks to mate with you."

"I love Dexar," I blurt out, and the room goes silent as the women stare at me in shock. It's true, I realize. On a planet where it would be so easy for him to become a merciless dictator, with so much power at his fingertips, he somehow remained *good.*

I clear my throat, glancing around the room at the women. "If all he wanted was prosperity for his tribe, he could've done exactly what Varic's doing now—forced me to mate with him as soon as we met. Instead, he protected me, giving me safety and letting me get to know him. Varic is the monster here."

I snap the last sentence, and Eagle Eyes steps closer.

"You will respect our qatai," she says.

"I respect those who have earned it. Your qatai is nothing more than a sad man who can't handle being number two, without the balls to be number one."

Eagle Eyes stares at me, her hand trembling, and I brace, well aware that she's about to slap me. I'm not going to fight a woman who looks like she could be in her sixties or seventies.

These people are like cult members. Varic has brainwashed them into believing that the prophecy is all they need for prosperity. That way, he doesn't need to do any of the work to actually create that prosperity, like, say, not pissing off the guy who practically runs this part of Agron.

The woman with the black hair steps forward, pulling Eagle Eyes away.

"You will bathe," the black-haired woman tells me, and I open my mouth to tell her to go fuck herself, but she continues, "There are many more of us than there are of you. If we have to strip you and clean you ourselves, we will."

I was wearing a thin blue dress when I was taken, and it's stained with Tavis's blood. I bet my face is also still bloody, and I'm suddenly desperate to be clean. I shrug. *Fine, then.*

The water is a little cooler than lukewarm, and I shiver as I cup my hands, rinsing my face. The women mostly ignore me, but they gasp and murmur amongst themselves when I flash them a glimpse of my tattoo as I reach for the towel.

One of the women gestures for me to sit on a wooden chair, and another begins working on my damp hair. From the feel of it, she's braiding it into an intricate design, which she's pinning on top of my head.

My stomach flutters with nerves. What if Dexar doesn't make it in time?

I blow out a shaky breath. He will. And if he doesn't, I'll get out of here myself. I almost snort at that. No one could accuse me of not being an optimist.

The women use some kind of Braxian makeup on my face, but I tune it all out. They chat quietly, and I create and discard escape plans like a child attempting origami. I'm only going to have one shot at this.

Finally, the women bring me a dress, and I roll my eyes as I examine it. The material may be a pure, bright white, but thanks to the low cut, my breasts will be lewdly on display. I grind my teeth.

From the little I've seen of this camp so far, it's obvious that the people here are living in poverty. They certainly aren't smelling too fresh, and a few of the women are currently staring at my bathwater as if they'd give anything to use it. Plus, all of the women in this kradi—including the one who is pregnant—look like they've been missing more than a few meals.

But Varic wasted money on a pretty costume so we can play dress up together and he can pretend to be a real king. Fury makes my hands shake as I reach for the dress, pulling it on without protest. I want to ask these women how much food could be bought with the delicate material, but what's the point?

Dexar lives in luxury, yes, but he ensures that no one in his tribe goes without. His warriors are ordered to keep an eye on everyone—from the most successful business owners to the oldest widows. Never would he allow his tribe to be hungry and grimy.

I'm so deep in thought that it takes a moment for me to realize that Eagle Eyes is gesturing for me to leave the kradi. The other women begin to file out, and the woman with the black hair glances back at my dirty bathwater with so much yearning that I could kill Varic for that alone.

Could I kill Varic?

I've never taken a life before. Beth told me that she and Nevada fought against both warriors from this tribe and the Voildi when they were defending Tecar's tribe. She said she killed more people than she could have imagined, and her eyes lowered at the admission. But when I asked her if she regretted it, she shook her head.

"Killing leaves a mark on you," she said. *"One that I think you carry for the rest of your life. But sometimes, some people*

have to die so that the innocent can live. I'm working on becoming okay with that."

She changed the subject, but I thought about her words that night as I got ready for bed. This is a brutal planet. I've seen sights here that I never could've imagined. I've had two attempts on my life in just a few weeks, and that's not counting the Voildi who were planning to eat us.

If I managed to take Varic out, could I live with myself afterward?

The pregnant woman makes a tiny sound, and I glance at her. She limps, and my gaze drops to her foot, which is bare on the rough ground. The women allowed me to put my own shoes back on, but all of them are barefoot, and I don't think it's because they hate the confinement of shoes.

Varic is pretending he's the ultimate leader, a tribe king that these people can trust. Meanwhile, they're obviously low on bare necessities like shoes, clothes, and food.

I stumble, raising a hand to my head as if I'm feeling woozy. One of the women grabs my elbow, and I slide a hairpin out of my hair, hiding it in my fist.

It feels heavy in my hand, with a surprising weight at one end where some kind of design has been carved into the metal. It's two-pronged, and the feel of the cool metal in my palm is reassuring even though it's unlikely to be much help.

The women lead me up a small hill to a grassy clearing. The sun has risen, and it's warm on the back of my neck. In any other situation, this setting would be oddly peaceful—the gush of the river is quieter here, broken by birdcalls and the sound of leaves rustling in the gentle breeze.

On the right, a huge fire burns, throwing off heat. The flames are climbing high, and a warrior is adding more wood as I watch.

Unfortunately, Varic is waiting for me—once again appearing unruffled. I wonder what his tribe would think if they'd seen him red-faced and ranting about Dexar, spittle flying from his mouth as he whined about being second best.

"Qatal," he says, smiling at me, and I roll my eyes. Members of his tribe surround us, and there must be two hundred people in this clearing alone. I have no doubt that Varic has more warriors posted outside the camp.

"I will never be your qatal," I say clearly, my voice carrying over the shocked gasps. "Look around this tribe. Look at the people you're supposed to be helping. You're not a qatai. You're a fucking disgrace."

His face slowly turns red, his eyes burning as he stares at me. "I thought you might feel that way." He smiles. "It's quite amusing, really. Dexar was so desperate to find you that he rode out of his camp gates, many of his most experienced warriors with him. Some of the youngest, most inexperienced warriors were left as sentries."

Varic turns his head, and I follow his gaze. Three of Dexar's warriors are hauled forward, all of them bruised and bleeding.

"Qatal." One of them nods respectfully, and I whirl, meeting Varic's eyes.

"Your disgust at Tavis's death proved you have a soft heart," he says. "I will simply cut pieces off these warriors until you behave."

He nods, and sone of his warriors slices a deep cut into the youngest warrior's bicep. He grits his teeth, and I'm the one who cries out.

"Stop!"

"Next, I'll take his arm." Varic smiles, his tone dripping

with smug satisfaction. He points at the ground in front of him, and I slowly walk forward.

My hands are unbound, but the idea of being able to escape this clearing is laughable. I glance to my right, and the bleeding warrior's eyes burn into mine as he silently shakes his head, urging me not to do this.

Varic holds two gold bands in his hands, and my heart suddenly hurts. I've seen those bands before, of course. They're for mated couples. Once they've been tenderly tied onto a woman's wrists by the man she loves, they're never removed.

Until this moment, I hadn't realized how much I'd secretly hoped to see Dexar holding those bands in his hands one day, a grin on his face as he winked at me.

I bite my lip until it aches. This asshole may think he can force me to mate with him, but I'll cut off those stupid bands at the first opportunity.

The warrior who led me from kradi to kradi moves forward, bowing his head at Varic respectfully.

"We have gathered to witness the mating of our qatai with his fated qatal. Through this mating, our tribe will be blessed by the gods with one hundred years of peace and prosperity."

The warrior smiles as the tribe cheers, and I scowl. Ini has a lot to answer for when it comes to that fucking prophecy.

I thought it would be easy to pretend that this means nothing. That I'd cut off these bands and annul this mating like a drunken Vegas wedding. And then Varic speaks.

Even his distant, robotic voice can't completely strip the meaning from his words.

"I have made these bands to represent our bond. Strong,

true, and never to be broken," he intones. "Will you accept them?"

I hesitate. Varic does not. He flicks his gaze to where Dexar's warriors are standing, and this time, one of them cries out. I turn, shrieking as one of Varic's warriors buries a knife in the young warrior's gut.

"You fucking asshole," I choke out as the warrior falls to his knees, the knife still flashing silver in his stomach.

Varic laughs, sounding genuinely amused. "You seem to believe that I am lying when I tell you the consequences of your actions."

I run my gaze over the crowd, lingering on the women, several of whom look pale.

"This is the qatai you follow?" I hiss. "The one you believe the fates will reward?" I laugh coldly, and several of the women drop their gazes.

Varic sighs, grabbing my shoulder and turning me toward him. "Enough dramatics. End this right now, or I will have all their throats slit."

I glance at the warriors. The other two have been gagged when I wasn't paying attention, but their eyes burn with fury. The warrior on the ground is groaning, his face gray.

This is it. As soon as Varic reaches for my wrists, it's going to be impossible for me to conceal the hairpin still clenched in my sweaty hand. The long sleeves of the dress currently hide it, but I have no doubt that this bastard will throw another murderous tantrum when he discovers it.

"Varic," a familiar sardonic voice says, and I whirl, a sob ripping from my throat. Dexar sits on his mishua wearing an honest-to-God *crown*, gleaming like fire in the sunshine. His clothes are immaculate, his expression mocking, but his eyes hold a promise of vengeance.

"It has been a long time." Dexar smiles, and I widen my

eyes as I realize how many of his warriors have managed to surround us. From the look of their blood-splattered clothes, they've taken down Varic's guards—quickly, effectively, and quietly.

This is Dexar at his best. No one looking at him would have any doubt that he's truly a king. He runs his eyes over the dusty, unkempt crowd, his raised eyebrow saying exactly what he thinks of them without uttering a word.

A rough hand clamps down on my shoulder, and I *know* Varic's about to use me as a shield. I twist back around as he bares his teeth, leaning down to hiss something at me.

I lash out, my hand reaching for him. The hairpin slashes across his face, surprising more than wounding, and he jolts back, his hands automatically releasing me.

I pivot, frantically scanning the clearing. Dexar's warriors attack, and swords clash as Varic's warriors leap into action.

Women are screaming, and I dart across the grass before Varic can grab me again. I reach the fire and lift one of the long sticks gathered next to it before thrusting the stick into the fire until it catches.

I hold it in front of me. It's the only weapon I have. The back of my neck tingles with awareness, and I turn to see Dexar stalking across the clearing toward me. Women are screaming and running out of the clearing, and warriors are fighting, but for one long moment, the rest of the world falls away as he reaches me.

"I knew you'd come for me."

He smiles at me, and his eyes seem to glow with vengeance as he looks over my shoulder.

"Brix is waiting for you." His eyes meet mine again, and he jerks his head to the right of the clearing, where there are no more of Varic's warriors left. Brix makes eye contact, and

I nod. Then, Dexar pulls me close, his lips hard on mine before he gently pushes me away.

He pulls the stick out of my hand and passes it to one of his warriors, who takes it back to the fire. Then he presses a long knife into my hand. "Go."

I turn my head, but I can't just run to safety. Not while that warrior is currently bleeding out. Dexar is already stalking to where Varic waits, his sword in his hand and retribution all over his face. His eyes meet mine for a moment, and I shiver at the hatred in them.

I bolt back across the clearing toward Dexar's sentries. The young warrior is still lying on the ground, his skin so pale that I'd think him dead if not for his twitching hand. The other two sentries have managed to get free, and they're fighting off Varic's warriors. One of them is the warrior who refused to help me—the one who ordered me from kradi to kradi—and I wince as Dexar's warrior drives him to his knees, burying his knife in his gut.

I drop to my own knees next to the young warrior, who cracks open his eyes as I brush his hair off his face.

"Qatal," he says, awe in his eyes, and I smile at him.

"Call me Alexis. What's your name?"

"Mika."

"Mika, you're going to be just fine, okay? Dexar will have brought healers with him, so you just have to hold on. Can you do that for me?"

He nods, but his eyes are closing again. I shudder as I notice the knife still buried in his stomach. Right now, it's acting like a cork, keeping him from bleeding out. If we can get him to a healer—or even better, bring the healer to him —he may just make it.

I huddle beside him, holding his hand. "Mika, stay with me, okay? Can you talk to me?"

He doesn't reply, and I glance up, my eyes darting around the clearing. There are just a few swords clashing now, and most of Varic's warriors have dropped their swords, well aware that they're outnumbered.

Dexar and Varic are fighting to the death. Varic bares his teeth and says something too low for me to catch. It's likely that he's hoping to piss Dexar off, but his face remains carefully blank. My heart is stuck in my throat, where it beats like a drum.

Varic swings his sword again, and Dexar simply steps to the side, saying something to Varic, his voice low as Varic's sword swings past him. I have a feeling Dexar's mocking him because Varic's face flushes and he swings again. Dexar dodges the blade, every movement smoothly economical, with no wasted effort.

I've seen Dexar train a few times, but the way he moves now...it's a thing of beauty. He's playing with Varic, allowing him to get tired even as Dexar steps forward, his arm lightning quick as he slashes across Varic's thigh.

The other man roars, and I shake as he swings his sword faster this time, slashing across Dexar's shoulder as he turns. Dexar punches him in the jaw, his knuckles hitting with a *crack* as he smoothly slides away, and I wince. That's gotta hurt. Varic's mouth hangs open, obviously dislocated.

I wince. The pain Varic's feeling right now must be unimaginable. I glance down at Mika, who hasn't regained consciousness, and just like that, I lose all sympathy for Varic.

Varic stumbles back, raising the hilt of his sword and slamming it into his own face, sliding his jaw back into place. Dexar doesn't wait, batting Varic's sword aside as Dexar raises his again, and he stops playing with him.

The sword slides into Varic's solar plexus. Dexar pulls it

free while Varic falls to his knees, and I close my eyes as Dexar swings his sword.

I swear I hear the thump of Varic's head as it hits the ground, but it's probably my imagination.

Dexar is immediately by my side, calling for a healer for Mika.

The warrior manages to open his eyes again, although they're blurry with pain. "Qatai."

"You have done well, Mika. Rest now. You will be healed and rewarded for protecting your qatal."

Brix appears, one of the healers by his side. I haven't been introduced to her, but I've seen her in the healers' kradi, and she nods at me as she kneels by Mika's side, opening her huge leather bag.

Dexar pulls me to my feet, cupping my face in his hands. "Are you okay?"

I blow out a long breath and begin to shake as the adrenaline leaves my body. Dexar's hands shift as his arms wind around me, and I bury my face in his chest.

"I am now," I say.

CHAPTER FIFTEEN

A lexis

I open my eyes, staring straight into achingly familiar forest green. The most incredible feeling of déjà vu immediately hits me. It's as if I've woken up the exact same way every day of my life.

"Were you watching me sleep, you creeper? You know, I've already had to deal with one stalker…"

A faint smile touches Dexar's mouth, but his eyes are still serious. "I have something to show you," he says. "Will you come with me?"

I raise an eyebrow at his cryptic tone, but his face is giving me no clues. We arrived back at camp last night, and after a quick bath, I fell into an exhausted sleep, curled up next to Dexar. When I woke in the middle of the night from a nightmare, he soothed me, stroking my hair until I fell back asleep.

"Of course." I reach for him, ready to snuggle. Okay, I'm ready for a lot more than snuggling. But Dexar simply winks at me, rolling out of bed and casting my bare skin one last look as he stalks out of the room.

I grin as he asks Yari for a cold bath.

It doesn't take me long to get ready, and before I know it, I'm pouting at Dexar as he insists on blindfolding me.

"Come on, is that really necessary?"

He simply winks at me again, holding out the blindfold. "Do you trust me?"

"I guess," I mutter sulkily, sticking out my lower lip. He strokes one finger across it, and then he's tying a soft cloth over my eyes.

The air is cool on my skin. My senses are heightened, and Dexar's warm body cradles mine as the mishua takes us who knows where.

If we were still in bed, I'd be more than happy to be blindfolded. My breath catches at the thought, and Dexar lets out a rough curse as if he knows exactly where my mind has gone.

I'm completely reliant on my other senses to figure out where I am. Dexar's guards murmur in low voices behind us, and I can't help but wonder if Dexar is returning me to Rakiz's tribe.

He's been acting strange since we arrived back at camp, holding me close and staring at me as if afraid I'll disappear. But he's refused to talk about *us* at all, and when I attempted to seduce him last night, he simply laughed at me.

To be fair, my eyes were half closed, and I was so tired I was slurring.

"Are we there yet?" I put on my whiniest voice, and Dexar laughs, pressing a kiss to my neck.

"Soon," he says, and I go back to enjoying the feel of the breeze on my skin.

I hear the rush of water, and I tense, the sound reminding me of Varic's camp. But Dexar's body is still relaxed against mine, and I lean my head back until it's resting against his hard chest.

I'm almost asleep by the time the mishua comes to a halt. I no longer hear Dexar's guards or the scuffling sound of the mishua behind us, so I'm guessing they're hanging back.

I'm strangely nervous, and I keep my eyes clamped shut for a moment longer while Dexar unties my blindfold.

"You can look now." His voice is amused, but I can hear a thread of nervousness, and it's this that makes me open my eyes.

My mouth drops open.

The spaceship sits on the riverbank, tilted drunkenly while one section leans precariously into the water.

It's shaped almost like a butterfly, with the tip of one wing dangling down, the cracked fuselage exposing a mess of wires like the innards of a dead animal.

Porthole windows are dotted at regular intervals along the side closest to us, and it's easy to imagine people staring out those windows as the ship plummeted to the ground.

The bottom half of the ship shows signs of rust, while the top still gleams silver like a new quarter.

I frown. A drop of liquid has just dripped from the ship and into the river. Perhaps some kind of fuel. It's bright orange and seems to glow, like the inside of a glow stick from Earth.

I'm instantly ready to explore.

"This is the ship that your father saw," I murmur. "The one that crashed before you were born."

I tear my gaze away from the ship as Dexar nods.

"I thought I wasn't *allowed* to come here," I say. My eyes widen as another thought occurs to me. "You're not going to have it destroyed, are you?"

"No." He sighs. "I'm not. Will you come with me? We will return, I promise."

I nod, and he moves back to the mishua before grabbing a large saddlebag. He takes the entire bag with him and reaches for my hand, walking me toward the edge of the forest and away from his guards.

One look from him and they stay where they are.

I'm ridiculously curious, but I bite my tongue as Dexar leads us out of sight of the guards and pulls a blanket out of the bag before laying it on the ground.

He gestures toward the blanket, and I raise my eyebrow as I sit down. Dexar is obviously nervous because he looks like he's itching to pace, although he sits next to me, his eyes dark.

"I was wrong to threaten to have the ships destroyed. I knew it the moment I said it. I never wanted to be someone you feared. I was afraid of losing you. The thought of never seeing you again..." His voice trails off, and I take a deep breath.

"Dexar—"

"Let me finish. Please."

I blink, unused to hearing that word come out of his mouth.

"I don't know if it's fate, or luck, or if there's another word that explains how you came to be here. With me. All I know is that from the moment I looked into your eyes, I knew that I wanted to keep looking into them for the rest of my life."

He glances away, and I open my mouth, stunned. Then

his eyes are fierce as he looks back at me, clenching his hands into fists.

"But perhaps you don't want to stay here. I was wrong to keep the prophecy from you, and I understand that you had a life on your planet." His lips twist ruefully, and I swallow around the sudden lump in my throat.

His voice is low, barely distinguishable. "My wishes are not more important than yours," he says simply. "I'd kneel at your feet if I thought it would convince you of my feelings for you. But you are, and have always been, your own person.

"So that is the ship. The ship that landed here so many years ago. You can examine it as many times as you want. And I'll also take you to the ship that brought you here so that you can compare them. If you choose to leave me, I will do whatever I can to help you get back to your home."

Dexar moves closer to me, his gaze suddenly tender as he raises his voice. "But if you choose to stay, I will never let you go. I will love and adore you until the end of our days."

I attempt to blink back my tears, but they spill over onto my cheeks anyway. Dexar looks as if I've punched him in the gut, his huge hand incredibly gentle as he wipes them from my cheeks.

"And what about the peace and prosperity for your tribe?" I ask.

Dexar squares his shoulders. "My tribe will have peace and prosperity regardless," he says haughtily. "I will ensure it."

I grin at him. There's my arrogant qatai.

We've come full circle, the tribe king and I. I tamp down my initial instinct to promise that I no longer want to go home, and instead, I take a moment to truly consider it.

Honestly, I miss it. I miss doing the kind of work I love, surrounded by like-minded people. The kind of people who were determined to figure out just how the Arcav had managed to sneak up on us, landing their ships in capital cities across the globe.

But you know what I'd miss more? The man standing in front of me, stripped back and vulnerable, his emotions completely exposed for me to see.

I take a deep breath. "You know, so many things had to happen for us to meet. I had to be abducted by aliens. I had to crash-land on this planet. I had to be in the group of women who were rescued by Terex. And then I had to volunteer to go to your tribe to learn about Charlie. I've never believed in fate. I guess I never wanted to believe that I was fated to be abandoned as a newborn." My voice tightens, and Dexar strokes his hand down the back of my hair.

I clear my throat. "But maybe now it's easier to believe that it *was* fate. That everything that happened to me was supposed to happen because it led me to you."

Dexar stills, and I'm struck by the hope in his eyes. His face is hard, his jaw like granite, but his hands reach for me before he fists them, dropping them to his sides.

"My whole life, I've been searching for somewhere to belong. And when I heard the prophecy, I was terrified by how much I wanted it to be true. By how much I wanted to belong with you and your tribe. Then I realized you'd kept it from me, and it felt like that hope was ripped away." My voice breaks, and I brush at the tears on my face. "I felt homesick when I was with Varic. Because after twenty-nine years of not having a home, I found one in just a few weeks. With you."

I sigh, staring up at the man who makes me feel *every-*

thing. Love, fury, sadness, lust, impatience, amusement—the whole range.

"Yes, I'll stay with you, Dexar. I don't want to be anywhere else."

My voice is muffled on the last word because Dexar has already pulled me into his arms, taking my mouth like he's drowning and I'm the only oxygen around. He buries his hand in my hair, his lips hard and insistent against mine, and I take everything he has to give, giving him everything I have in return.

Mine. This incredibly handsome, frustrating, imperious tribe king is mine.

And God I want him.

I pull away, pressing kisses along the sensitive spots beneath his jaw. He shudders against me, and I smile.

Within moments, I'm flat on my back, blinking up at him as he rips off his clothes. He's gentle with me, kissing along my collarbone before pulling my dress down until my arms are trapped by my sides.

"Hey," I grumble, and he grins, kissing along my shoulders, my breasts and paying particular attention to my tattoo as he nuzzles my dress out of the way.

I work one hand free and bury it in his hair, urging him back up. We kiss again, my nipples hard against his chest, and then he pulls away, his eyes so dark they appear almost black.

My dress is gone an instant later, and I gaze around us. I've never made love outside before, and I feel suddenly vulnerable.

"No one would dare interrupt us," Dexar murmurs, and I grin up at him.

"Of course they wouldn't."

I no longer care about anything except him, and I moan as he reaches down, stroking along my damp folds.

"Hurry up, damn you."

Dexar tuts, but his muscles are shaking as he pushes one finger inside me, and he growls as I clamp around him.

"So impatient." He thrusts inside me, hard, hot, and deep. His body cradles mine, and I no longer care about anyone who could possibly be stupid enough to sneak up behind us.

He moves deeper, angling his thrusts to hit the spot that makes me toss my head and groan. He chuckles, and I crack open my eyes, staring up at him. His eyes seem luminescent as the breeze parts the branches of the trees above us and the sun dances across his face.

My thighs begin to shake, my nipples so tight that they're achy, and he changes his angle again, this time grinding against my clit as he hits that same spot deep inside me.

My wave of pleasure crests, and everything stops as I contract around him, gasping as he continues his steady thrusting, dragging out my pleasure. Finally, he growls, shuddering against me, and buries his face in my neck.

He's careful not to crush me, but we lie for long moments, catching our breath as I stroke the smooth muscles of his back.

"It won't be an easy life by my side," he murmurs. "People watch me constantly, and they will likely begin to bring their problems to you as well. You will know little privacy and even less peace. But I will do everything I can to ensure you never regret choosing to stay with me."

My heart melts. He's still trying to make sure I know what I'm in for.

"Trying to make me change my mind?"

"Never. Just preparing you."

"I told you, Your Majesty, I'm all in."

Dexar pulls his head back, staring down at me. "You'll never regret it," he tells me. "I promise."

I grin. What do a scrappy foster kid and an alien king have in common?

Love.

A lexis

One week later

I stare at the ship, my stomach fluttering as Dexar takes my hand in his.

We couldn't hang around here for long last week, since Dexar needed to be back at the tribe to deal with the remaining people from Varic's tribe. Unsurprisingly, many of his people were impressed with the way Dexar showed up in all his royal magnificence. The fact that his warriors took out Varic's guards within a few moments must have left an impression as well because many of those same people have been petitioning to join us.

After what happened with Tavis, Dexar was understandably hesitant, but one glance at the barefoot women had him heaving a sigh and throwing up his hands.

Now he's arranging for most of them to be integrated into our tribe.

"It's strategic," he told me firmly when I praised him.

"Uh-huh. You keep on telling yourself that, big guy."

It's just one of the things I adore about him. As much as he likes to play the part of the ruthless bastard, Dexar has a soft, squishy core.

Of course, even I only get to see that part of him occasionally.

Not all the warriors chose to stay with Dexar's tribe. Some of them moved on to form their own tribe, while others left alone to either petition other tribes or live a lone-wolf life. Either way, it took some time to organize those who chose to stay. They were given positions within the tribe where they can be easily watched until they've built up enough trust to be allowed to stay with no strings attached.

Dexar apologized repeatedly, saying that he'd bring me back here as soon as he could. Now we're both examining the silver ship, Dexar's eyes narrowed on it suspiciously.

"It's difficult to believe that you landed here on a ship like that."

"I know. It almost seems impossible to me now." After spending so long on a planet as uncivilized as Agron, the ship stands out like a movie prop against the lush green grass and clear blue water.

I frown at the river, where drops of that bright-orange fluid continue to drip occasionally into the clear water. Braxians get their drinking water from rivers across Agron, although they boil it before drinking.

"Dexar," I say suddenly, "is this the river that you guys use for drinking water?"

He nods. "This river comes from those mountains, and the water is clear and pure. Our ancestors made their camps near this river, and most Braxian tribes continue this tradition today."

I stare at the ship some more, letting go of Dexar's hand to pace.

I don't like seeing the ship sitting in the river we use for drinking and bathing water. But how do we remove it?

There's just one part of the ship in the water. What we need is something huge to push against it and drag it up onto the bank.

Something like a dragon. Maybe the dragon is actually friendly? And maybe it wouldn't mind doing us a teeny little favor?

He folds his arms. "What are you thinking?"

"It sounds crazy, but hear me out, okay?"

He nods.

"I have no idea what that orange fluid is. But here's what I do know: Thirty-eight years ago, Elliz's mom began to notice that there were fewer female babies being born. This got progressively worse over the years."

"Yes."

"Forty years ago, this ship crash-landed here. No one has touched it, right?"

"No one from my tribe. I do not know about the other tribes."

I nod. "Okay, I need a few minutes."

Dexar nods, planting himself on the grass in the sun while I watch the liquid until I finally see it drip. "One Mississippi, two Mississippi..." I count until I get to 178.

Three minutes. That's how long there is between drops. I count again just to be sure, wishing I had a stopwatch or even a wristwatch right now.

Dexar is sprawled in the sun, his eyes heavy-lidded as he watches me.

"I just need a few more minutes."

"Take your time."

I walk back to the mishua, where Dexar's guards are waiting. They nod at me, returning to their conversation as I reach into the saddlebag and pull out my paper and pencil.

I walk back to Dexar and sit cross-legged next to him in the sun as I scribble my calculations.

One drop every three minutes is approximately 480 drops per day. If the liquid has a consistency similar to water, it's a little over eleven gallons a year. Multiply that by forty...

I stare at Dexar, and he raises an eyebrow.

"Four hundred and fifty gallons," I murmur.

"Excuse me?"

"If this thing has been dripping since the crash, there has been around four hundred and fifty gallons of whatever weird space liquid that is dumped in this water."

Dexar's eyes narrow. "Is this a large amount?"

I shrug. "Depends on whatever the hell that liquid is. If it's some kind of fuel, it may not be too bad—but what do I know about the type of space fuel used by people on other planets? I'd expect a ship that size to have hundreds of thousands, if not millions, of gallons of fuel. But if it's something dangerous..."

Dexar frowns, and I blow out a breath.

"I think that it's very interesting that whatever is in that ship has been dripping into your drinking water for as long as there have been fewer females born on this part of the planet."

Dexar's eyes flare, and I hold up a hand.

"Look. Correlation is not causation. The two things may be completely unconnected. But for now, we know that something new has been added into your water supply. The problem is that we don't know *when* this stuff started dripping from the ship. Did it happen recently? Or was it happening the whole time?"

"There were three warriors who found this ship with my father. Many other warriors have visited it over the years. We can ask if they noticed it."

I nod. "Maybe—"

"Alexis?"

I spin, my mouth dropping open until I probably look like a fish. A woman is running toward me, a huge smile on her face.

No way.

"Charlie?"

The last time I saw her, I was seriously worried about her head wound. If she were on Earth, I would've called an ambulance, but instead, she had to walk for hours with us as we followed the Voildi.

Now she looks great. Her skin is flushed with health, and she's moving easily, her eyes sparkling.

I clamp my hands over my ears as the ground seems to shake. Something's roaring, but it sounds like thunder, and I glance at the guards, who all cringe, covering their own ears. Dexar lunges in front of me, pushing me behind him and drawing his sword as the dragon lands.

It's huge.

Dexar's guards step in between us and the dragon, their swords raised in front of them.

The beast is beautiful. Blue-green scales gleam like polished jewels in the sunlight, and his sheer power and strength is displayed as he bunches his muscles, crouching next to Charlie. He spreads his wings, displaying the incredible array of colors and shades spanning the entire spectrums of blues and greens.

His eyes are gold, hooded, and cunning as he examines us, the tilt of his head making it clear that he's unimpressed by what he sees. He steps forward, each incremental move saturated with threat as his muscles seem to roll. His chest is like a barrel as he tucks his wings closer.

Then he opens his mouth, displaying rows upon rows of sharply pointed teeth. He blows out a small flame, almost like a hiccup, but the warning is obvious.

Next to him, Charlie looks at me and throws up her hands in a "what are you gonna do" motion. The dragon takes another step forward, and the juxtaposition between the cool, soothing colors of his scales and the flames that he can spit at any moment is clear.

The good news? Charlie is alive. The bad news? She's obviously being held prisoner by a fiercely aggressive dragon.

I grind my teeth, frustrated.

"Are you okay?" I call to Charlie, and she steps closer. The dragon doesn't like this, and I clamp my hands over my ears again as he roars once more. His tail is a whip that lashes the ground, communicating that he will be taking no shit.

My heart is racing, and Dexar pushes me back further, throwing me a look that suggests I shut the hell up. I scowl at him but clamp my mouth shut.

Charlie says something as she turns, glowering at the dragon. My mouth drops open again as she bops him on the snout with her fist. He snorts, smoke curling from his nose, as he narrows those dinner-plate-sized eyes at her.

Okay, then.

"I'm fine!" she yells across the space. "But—"

The dragon has clearly had enough because he shoots us one last look and wraps the claws of one foot around

Charlie, scooping her up. He keeps his foot tilted flat, and she lands on her butt on top of his foot, waving at me as the dragon launches from the ground, spreading his wings in flight.

He's like a fucking rocket, and he's gone in seconds.

The part of me that's obsessed with aerodynamics wants to watch that again.

The part of me that's terrified of being eaten by a dragon wants to find somewhere to hide.

I turn to Dexar. "Told you she was alive."

He rolls his eyes, but his lips twitch as he pulls me close, kissing me on the forehead. "Indeed."

The one from the stars is fated to arrive
Born distantly, with those of her kind
White of hair and light of eyes
Destined for the qatai to find.

When mated three revolutions and one day
Peace will spread throughout the land
An eternal love, never to be betrayed
For one hundred years, prosperity will stand.

The End

Thank you for reading Seduced by the Alien Warrior! If you enjoyed it and you have a few moments to write a review with your thoughts, I'd sooo appreciate it!

Want to be the first to know about freebies, new releases and sales? Sign up for my free newsletter here.

Ivy and Vrex are up next in Protected by the Alien Warrior. Things are heating up for this firefighter and her mercenary alien warrior so be sure to check it out!